Thistle Creek

Vanna Tessier

Thistle Creek

A COLLECTION OF NEW SHORT STORIES

EDMONTON
SNOWAPPLE PRESS

Snowapple Press
Box 66024, Heritage Postal Outlet
Edmonton, Alberta, T6J 6T4

Canadian Cataloguing in Publication Data

Tessier, Vanna
Thistle Creek

ISBN 1-895592-23-2

I. Title.
PS8589.E8284T54 2000   C813'.54   C99-911183-3
PR9199.3.T436T54 2000

"Snow Apple" -- a North American variety of apple having red-streaked fruit.

∞ACID FREE PAPER - Recycled paper produced with the alkaline
process of papermaking, resulting in a **non-acid**, environmentally friendly
product that has long lasting, non-fading archival properties. The paper used in
this publication should meet the requirements for permanence of paper for
Printed Library Materials.

First Printing, 2000

1 2 01 00

MANUFACTURED AND PRINTED IN CANADA

CONTENTS:

PART ONE:

PART TWO:

TO THOSE WHO DARE SWIM AGAINST THE CURRENT.

Acknowledgments

For supporting my research and for encouraging me to continue my work over the years, I wish to thank Canada Council and the staff of The Edmonton Public Library, always willing to promote my writing and to launch my books.

Some of these stories have appeared in a different form:

MY TOUGH TEETH, performed at the Yardbird Suite Spring Festival; AWAKENING, Edmonton Journal Literary Award; I CAN'T COMPLAIN, broadcast on CBC Radio.

Cover Art & Graphics
By G. H. Tessier

Thistle Creek

Part One

THISTLE

"Damn!" Karyn stumbles over a mound of dirt. "It's too quiet here. Nobody's around!" As she increases her pace, purple-thorned thistles brush against her leg. "It's spooky. That's all I need. Is he not home? I can hear Thistle Creek splash and gurgle deep down in the narrow gorge. Used to go skinny-dipping there in the summer. Scraped my skin raw." She sucks in her lower lip and with her sleeve she dries the blood from the long scratch on her leg.

She waddles through a wide puddle, reaching the aspen tree which watches over the grey-stuccoed house at the end of the gravel road. The rust-gnawed Plymouth is not parked at its usual place on the driveway. Karyn grinds her teeth.

"Where is my car? Jesus! Too bad I let Thistle drive it. He insisted he needed it." She stares at the windows of the house to see if anyone is at home. All the brown-fringed curtains are drawn, like eyelids shut tight. "Something is wrong. Did he take the car again? Rats! Let's see if he still has his garden in the backyard."

She climbs the steps to the wooden porch. The boards creak under her feet as if her body weighed a lot more than fifty kilos. Jerking her arm back, she pulls the screen door open. The walnut door is locked. She fumbles under the black rubber mat for the spare key, but she can't find it. She searches in her purse for her ring of car keys. The house key is missing. If she could pick the lock, she might be able to get in. A credit card comes in handy and does the trick. The door squeaks open. The stale, stuffy air at the entrance hits her face as if the house were breathing on her. Karyn steps back and sighs. Smells of smoke and dirty socks linger in the hallway. In a corner, a potted plant lets its wilting leaves fall to the floor like corn flakes. Crumpled papers and cigarette butts litter the faded carpet in the living room. Someone had left in a hurry. From the ceiling, a bare bulb hangs livid similar to a bruised eye.

In the kitchen, the sink is full of dirty dishes. Not one clean plate is left inside the cupboard. Not a clean cup or saucer. Not even a decent glass to drink from. Greasy salad bowls, sticky mugs and tumblers are piled up high. It's like him to leave filthy pots and burnt-black frying pans stacked almost to the ceiling. Rather than wash messy platters and ashtrays, he abandons them everywhere.

Karyn turns on the tap. She squirts blue liquid detergent in the warm water to wash the dishes, but some drops splash onto her pale green dress. A belt of dark polka dots marking her waist. She wipes her hands with a dish cloth and tries to rub the stubborn stains dry. She ties a cotton apron around her hips, picks up a dusty mop and soaks its fuzzy head into the murky water of a plastic pail. She should have asked Thistle to scrub the grime streaking the linoleum floor in the hallway leading to the bedroom.

She rummages through a chest of drawers and finds a photo album open with the picture of a white-veiled bride who trembles as she cuts the first frosted layer of a wedding cake. Thistle's fleshy hand covers hers in the photo. She wanted to slice the cake for both, but forks and spoons clinked against thin-necked wineglasses until she brushed back the white veil from her face. Thistle kissed her. He searched for her tongue and she couldn't breathe. The rough stubble on his chin poked into her skin. He had shaved in the morning, but his bristles grew faster than weeds and he couldn't get rid of them. That was why Karyn called him Thistle. She thought he would stick by her and, at his side, she might become tough-skinned like him. When he kissed her, he would often pinch her as if to brand her with his seal of approval. But she didn't expect to be pinched among the guests at her wedding reception. The sharp sting of pain caught her by surprise. Karyn couldn't move away from him. Thistle was hugging her with both arms. He squeezed her, but didn't make a move to reach for her bum. Who would have the nerve to pinch her bottom on her wedding day? The gall.

She glanced around and caught Thistle's older brother Khriss grinning. His fast fingers groped amid the lacy pleats of her creamy white gown as if he knew what he was doing. She didn't want to make a big fuss about that. A mountain out of a molehill.

The brawny Khriss had eyed her with longing from the first time he met her. Maybe he hoped to go out with her, but he never asked her for a date. Thistle ignored his jealous brother and couldn't see anything wrong if the three of them went out together. Often, Thistle invited his older brother to go to the movies with them on Saturday. Khriss hugged Karyn as if she would soon join their family and he could do what he wanted with her.

She could not forget the time when Thistle took her for a picnic on the bank of Thistle Creek. She put down the basket with the egg sandwiches and he tickled her until they both rolled down the grassy embankment to the rushing water of the creek. She felt light headed, as if she could take chances. She bounced on the grassy slope. Emptiness seemed to suck her in and she thought she was caught in a whirlpool. A funnel of air. Was she falling? Falling in love? They flipped onto the creek bed, soaking wet like a couple of school kids washing their sweat off after a romp in a haystack. Cool. Slippery. The wind blew hard and let them enjoy each other's warmth.

Thistle, tightlipped, became interested in growing pot. He would sweat in the backyard, watching the green plants grow tall and lush. At times, he would also work on the car and when he came in, the house would smell of oil and rotten eggs. Karyn got tired of waiting for him. She found a job cleaning and washing dishes for a wealthy family. But after a few weeks, Thistle didn't let her go to work. He wanted her to help him water his plants.

"Not too much trouble with marijuana. Only hope. Freedom. Mary Jean is understanding. She never complains. Makes me dream," he would tell Karyn. He called the tallest plant in his garden Mary Jean, or MJ, as if it were a woman he could make love to.

Karyn began feeling jealous. Mary Jean was always available, never tired and Thistle knew where to find her in the dark. The plants grew luscious and bright green like festive Christmas trees. If he was short of money, Thistle would offer a pinch of Mary Jean to his brother Khriss who began visiting them more often. He would stay in the house sipping tea with Karyn, while Thistle spent more time in the garden with Mary Jean.

One evening Khriss rode his black and chrome motorcycle up the driveway. He found Thistle passed out on the loveseat under the influence of Mary Jean. Khriss scouted through the fridge for some leftovers and then grabbed Karyn, shoved her into a corner and pinned her against the wall. He reached down and pinched her bum hard. The rancid smell of garlic on his breath and his stinking greasy hair made her sick. She threw up on his shirt and he let her go. Barefoot, she ran outside. She didn't even return to pick up the rest of her clothes until two months later.

She looked for a job as a waitress. But she was starting at the bottom of the ladder and washing dishes at the *Bees & Berries Restaurant* was the only work she could find. The head dishwasher made eyes at her.

"Could get ahead if you go out with me," he told her, but she glanced away.

Sure, she wanted to look for a better paying job. She didn't like the basement suite she shared with clambering cockroaches and squirming silverfish. She couldn't afford to leave her old Plymouth parked at back.

Thistle met her at the *Bees & Berries* one evening when he decided to eat out for a change. His fingernails were rimmed with grime and the bristles of his stubble were darker than usual, hardly masking his grin as he waved Karyn over to his table. She was wearing a blue smock and couldn't deny she was working there. She wanted to talk to him about picking up her car at his place, but she couldn't leave the restaurant until after midnight.

Karyn was curious. She wanted to find out whether the police had visited the house Thistle rented near the city limits. Leaving him alone with Mary Jean had not been the best for Thistle. Karyn was not sure if she could do something for him, but she vowed to help him behave.

A car screeches to a halt outside. Could this be Thistle returning home? Karyn looks out the front window. It is her car, no doubt about that. Thistle might step out any minute now. Only a striking champagne blonde hops out of the car, shuts the door and straightens her paisley sapphire skirt. Swinging her hips, the woman heads for the house.

With long strides, the blonde struts over tufts of burnt brown quack grass poking out of the cracks in the driveway. She manages to slip past a nest of prickly thistle. A curry fox terrier wobbles behind her as the loose boards of the front porch squeak.

The woman's hair flaps with a sudden gust of wind, a wing brushing the side of her head. The fox terrier sniffs around her feet. She reaches for the doorknob and turns it as if she knew it would be unlocked.

When she steps into the living room, the dog sneaks in too. The animal wags its hairy tail, nuzzling the stand of the brass lamp in the corner. The terrier snaps back, lifts a hind leg and sprays.

"No! Idiot! Stupid dog!" Karyn stomps into the room, her eyes bulging out of their sockets. "Getting out of hand, huh? What a beast!"

"This your dog?"

"No. No." She waves her hand and twitches her eyebrows as the blonde bends over and reaches for the fox terrier's neck.

"Watch it, boy. Back up." The blonde drags the animal away. "You're going to get it."

"Hey! Don't bother the poor thing," Karyn shouts. She shakes her head. "How could you let him piss on the rug?"

"Didn't."

Karyn glares at the stain around the stand of the brass lamp. "Thought you'd know better than bring in a damned dog like that one."

"Found him down the road. It chased the car, barking. Followed me and here I am."

"That doesn't mean the dog belongs here."

"Doesn't it?" The woman slaps some dust off a padded chair. "Hummph!" She coughs. "Just as dirty as the car seat. Wasn't that bad before."

"Before?"

"Yeah! When I drove that car myself."

"What do you mean *when* you drove that car?" Karyn places her fists on her hips. "You never touched that Plymouth until you drove it here."

"Sure did."

"No way. Couldn't be. Like an intruder. Dragging in that filthy dog. Pissing all over. Phew! Wrecking everything." Karyn crosses her arms. "Now you say you drove my Plymouth. Who are you?"

"I'm Kheyla."

"And what are you doing here?" Karyn steps away from a platform of red brick tiles where a black potbellied wood burning stove sits next to an aluminum pan stuffed to the rim with grey ashes.

Kheyla strolls by the stove. Her paisley skirt fans the ashes which spill over into a flurry of grey specks flying around like moths. She watches them as if hypnotized. The fox terrier barks, racing after the grey-winged swarm.

She swings her leather handbag over her left shoulder. "Thought I'd drop in. That noisy mutt tagged along. Could be yours. You never know."

"Told you! Don't have a dog."

"This friendly fox terrier showed me the way here. Feels at home in this place."

The animal sniffs around the padded chair and trots to the wall near the coffee table. It bites the plug of the lamp.

"Hey! Don't eat that plug." Karyn is worried. "Stupid animal."

"Sure knows where everything is."

The dog growls and pulls the plug out from the wall. Sparks shoot around like fireflies looking for a mate on a warm summer night.

"Stop it! That beast doesn't fit in here." Karyn points her index finger at the blonde Kheyla. "Neither do you."

"Why not? Think you do?" Kheyla presses her lips tight and frowns.

"Don't have to tell you anything." Karyn could feel the sharp sting of jealousy. She came to talk to Thistle. Where could he be? Why would this woman drive up in *her* car? How could Thistle let a stranger drive *her* car home? Kheyla maybe took the Plymouth for a joyride, but she knew where he lived. Did she ever visit him here before?

She had arrived just out of the blue, like an alien invader with a pet. Karyn didn't want to let the woman snoop around the house as if she owned it. This was where she used to live herself as a bride not long ago. She wouldn't allow Kheyla too close to the bedroom where she cuddled up to Thistle each evening. Even if this champagne blonde would call on him, it wouldn't matter. Thistle would not fall for the fine chiseled features and the curvaceous body of this freckled-faced creature, would he?

Showing off the tip of a scarlet wrinkled tongue, the terrier is nosing around Kheyla's ankle. She doesn't mind the dog licking her nylons. "Let's go, Ruff! We should find something better than this pigpen."

Karyn's face turns hot pink. "How dare you say such a thing?"

"Don't you ever clean or tidy up this dumpy place?" Kheyla sweeps aside a fringe of hair from her forehead. "I mean, if you live here, you should look after this house."

"What do you care if I live here or not?"

"Haaawright! Didn't know I'd find you here."

"There are many things you don't know." Karyn doesn't want to tell the woman about her problems. Kheyla might be Thistle's friend. Or a spy. An undercover cop.

"Yeah, sure!" The woman clenches her fists. She grins, baring her polished teeth as sharp and shiny as those of a saw. "Can't leave this poor animal stay here in such a mess. It's not fit for a dog. Poor thing! It could get hurt stepping on a nail, or something."

"Who said that bitch could stay here?" Karyn squints, her eyelids quivering.

"Call the pound then."

The terrier sniffs the air and scurries away. A car door slams shut outside. A child begins to cry.

Karyn turns her head. "Whaaaat the heck . . . ."

"Wait!" Kheyla rushes to the front door. She scrambles down the wooden steps.

A red-faced toddler stretches his chubby little arms out of the window of the rusty Plymouth. "Maaaahhh!"

In his acid-rinsed bluejeans and a black-striped shirt, a muscular man rolls up his sleeves, showing off his biceps.

"Don't cry now, kiddo." He strokes the light fuzz on the child's head.

The toddler shrieks louder. "Maaaaahh!"

Kheyla catches her breath and shoves the man's hand aside. "Get away from my son. You!" she gasps. "Don't you dare bother my child, Thistle. Should report you." She loosens the strings of her leather handbag and rummages inside. "Here, my pet!" She hands a chocolate chip cookie over to the toddler who starts nibbling at it.

"Didn't know you had a kid," Thistle says.

"You never asked." Kheyla picks up her child. She brushes a few crumbs from his round chin and she glances up at Thistle, as if to show him who is the boss.

"Won't ask you out anymore." He shrugs.

"Right, Flipper! That sounds like a good idea." Karyn joins them. She slaps Thistle's shoulder. "Are you two up to your dirty tricks again?"

"Karyn!"

"What's up? Better tell me the truth. How did you get here?"

"Had to walk all the way home. Someone took the Plymouth." Thistle stretches out his arm and he glares at Kheyla. "Think it's her!"

"It's my car," Kheyla shouts. The child squirms in her arms and purses his lips. She places the toddler on the front seat.

"How could that be?" Karyn stands between them like a policeman directing traffic. "It's mine."

"No way!" Kheyla snaps. "It can't be."

When Karyn elbows Kheyla's ribs, she staggers against the side of the car. "Ask Thistle!" Karyn shouts. "He'll tell you it's mine."

"Don't even bother asking." Thistle shakes his head, as if he wants to forget about the Plymouth.

"Why did you let this woman drive my car?" Karyn stamps her foot. With her fist, she jabs his chest. "Why?"

"Left it with the motor running in front of the grocery store. Wouldn't ever let anyone else drive your car. You know that, Karyn."

"Went in for cigs, huh?" Karyn rasps.

"So? What's that to you?" Thistle scowls.

"You don't care about the car, because it's not yours." Karyn slaps her palm on the Plymouth's hood.

"Sure do. But when I came out of the store, the old rusty clunker was gone." Thistle folds his arms. "Looked all over. Ran up and down the street. Thought a kid went for a joyride."

"Had this car more than a year ago." Kheyla nods, glancing at the Plymouth. "It's mine." She pats the child's rosy cheeks dry.

"Did you sell it? Or something?" Thistle twitches his lips.

"Never did."

"Maybe it wasn't this clunker. Just a car that looked the same as this one," Thistle says.

"It's this one for sure. I should know. And so should you." Kheyla scowls.

"Bought this wreck from a man who cooked up a deal." Thistle lifts the wipers and cleans some leaves from the windshield.

Karyn steps up to Thistle and shakes her fist near his face. "It's all your fault. See what kind of trouble you cause me? I didn't want to buy that vehicle. That man who was selling it was too much in a hurry."

"But it was a bargain. You didn't have much money. What else could you buy?"

"That shouldn't be the reason to go for the first car you see." Karyn punches Thistle's chest and he grabs her fist.

"Want to fight?" He squeezes her wrist and tightens his grip until she grimaces.

"Hey, let go of me!" Wrenching her wrist from his fingers, Karyn steps back. "I worked hard for that money."

"What's the big deal?" Kheyla sighs and the toddler grabs a strand of her blond hair. "The Plymouth was stolen when I parked it in a dim-lit area at a viewpoint. Off Thistle Creek. Went down the ravine to dip my feet in the creek. When I came back, the car was gone."

Karyn tugs at Thistle's arm. "That's why the man who sold me the car was in such a hurry. He wouldn't take a cheque. Wanted hard cash. Right then. Had to cough it up on the spot."

"Report the crook." Kheyla shoves back long strands of hair. "A thief belongs in jail."

"But how can we find him? We don't even know where he lives." Karyn rolls her eyes around.

"Is that possible? Didn't you go to his house to look at the car for sale?"

"No. He drove all the way here to meet us," Thistle says. "He might have skipped town by now."

Kheyla knits her eyebrows together and glowers at him. "And how come you never showed up at work with the Plymouth? Tried to hide it?"

Thistle kicks some gravel with the steel tip of his boot. "The engine conked out on me when I started work. Just left that stinker at the garage. But they were too busy to repair it. Spent a lot of money on that clunker. Gas-guzzler." He kicks in a rust spot on the lower body of the car.

"Don't complain about that. You drove around until it broke down." Karyn wipes the side mirror and adjusts it. "You never took care of my car."

Kheyla leaves her child on the front seat. She twists to one side as Karyn grabs her arms. She jerks back to free herself. She punches Karyn's jaw hard, but can't avoid a powerful blow to her ribcage. Bent over, Kheyla covers her breasts with her hands. Karyn pommels her shoulder blades with both fists. She doesn't stop beating and hammering even when Thistle whistles loud, doing the count as if he were witnessing a boxing match.

Kheyla's eyelids look red and swollen, but she doesn't cry. A rush of adrenaline shoots through her body like a sudden blast of energy. She aims her forehead at Karyn. An enraged bull attempting to poke a matador with its horns.

"Maaahhh!" The child cries.

"Girls!" Thistle clutches Karyn's arms to break up the struggle. "Enough." Kheyla strikes his bristly chin. Caught between the two of them, Thistle tugs and shoves to stop the fist fight.

"Get lost, dammit!" hisses Karyn, swaying to one side like a drunk. "Let me fight my own battles. You sure owe me that much."

A roaring motorcycle drives up, bounces over the curb and spits fumes at the Plymouth until the engine screeches to a halt. The black-helmeted motorcyclist jumps off.

"Hey, guys! Wait for me if you want a good fight," he yells. His strong, rough hands clutch Karyn's waist. "Giving you a tough time, hah? Brother. Thistle deserves more than hell."

"What are you doing here, Khriss?" Thistle whacks his brother's arm. "Leave her alone. She's not married to you."

"You're crazy to let this girl live out there by herself." Khriss puts his arm around Karyn's shoulders. "Don't stare at me with those emerald eyes. They're precious." He winks at her. "Why don't you come home with me, little sister? Could look after you real good."

"No." Karyn shrinks away fast enough for Khriss to bump into Kheyla.

"Watch what you're doing." Kheyla shoves him aside before shuffling away. "Don't bother me."

Karyn pushes back Kheyla who crashes against Khriss again. "Go home with her. Bum. Spending your life on a motorcycle. You eat and sleep on it. Don't have time to work. And you make Thistle sell pot."

The child screams. "Mahhhh!"

"A minute, Jess! You're right." Kheyla steps closer to the front of the car. "We'll just drive away. Just you and me.

Have my own problems. Never mind other people's."

Karyn blocks her way. "You are *not* going anywhere. This car stays here with me. It's mine."

Kheyla bends over and snaps open the glove compartment which yawns with its dark mouth. She wipes off some dust and she points at the letters carved on the inside of the small door. "Look! I scratched my name right here."

Thistle stares at the carved letters. "Never noticed that before."

"It doesn't mean anything." Karyn stomps away.

"Looks like we'll have to let you drive this wreck until it falls apart." Khriss grins, showing off his crooked yellow teeth. "Too bad, hah!"

"It won't break." Kheyla strokes the side of the car and opens the driver's door.

"If you let me drive it for a few days, I'll fix the brakes for you. Free of charge. What do you think?" Thistle says, looking over her shoulder.

Karyn jumps between them. She punches Thistle's side. "You don't need to drive my car. Get your own."

"Yeah! Sell a few joints and get some money to buy your own bike." Khriss smacks his lips and slaps Thistle's shoulder. "How about smoking it up? Before the cops catch up to us?"

"Cops? Who wants some dumb cops around?" Thistle whistles between his teeth. He clenches his jaw as if he had to face a court decision sending him to jail. "You're joking? Don't even mention any cops, or they might show up at your door step."

Khriss spits and wipes his mouth with the back of his hand. "Saw the blue-striped cruiser at the other end of the road."

"Why did you come here? To bother me, or what?"

Thistle shouts and shakes his fist. "You can't just lead them straight to my place. Idiot!"

"Didn't. The cruiser was speeding, chasing after a wine coloured van. Fuzz catching a speeder, I guess. Thought the cops ogled me on my bike."

"That's suspicious. Shady. They might get you sooner or later." Thistle threatens his brother with one fist. "You deserve to be locked up forever."

"I'd rather crash against a wall than end up in jail." Khriss waves at his motorcycle. "That's freedom. Fresh air." He steps closer to his bike. "Think I'll go now."

Thistle grabs his arms. "No. You don't. The cops might be here soon."

"They won't find me. Don't worry."

"Moron. Bet they want to grab your bike." Thistle is perspiring and he wipes his forehead with his hand. "You're in trouble. Smoking pot and everything." He glances around as if afraid to see people he doesn't want to meet.

Kheyla wipes her child's tears. She shakes her head. "Didn't know you smoke ash, Thistle." She sighs. "You're not the man I thought you were."

"And who are you? People change all the time." Thistle stares at the child who still sobs. "Look at your tot."

"Awwright!" Kheyla smacks her lips. "You know all about raising children?"

Thistle stretches out his arm and strokes the cheek of the child. "Sure could learn."

"You've got some growing up to do. I see." Karyn leans against the Plymouth.

The toddler drops his cookie and whimpers as Kheyla screams, "Get away from him. Don't scratch my child with your awful beard."

Thistle fingers the stubble on his chin. "What I do is

always wrong. Women! Wish you'd make up your mind."

"You lie. Took my car," Kheyla shouts. "You're not the same fellow I hung out with. Can't trust you."

"I can change myself." Thistle scratches the bristles on his chin. "But can't change what you think of me. Or anyone else." He bends over the seat to pick up the cookie the child had dropped.

Kheyla shoves Thistle back and yells, "Don't you dare touch him! Stay away from my kid." She turns around as Khriss steps closer to the car. "Hey! Who pinched me?" Her face becomes scarlet. She opens her mouth wide as if about to scream for help.

"Not me." Khriss grabs her arm and places her hand on his chest. "Cross my heart."

"Heh! Get away from me," she hisses at him, trying to wrench her arm free. She pommels him with her other fist.

"How would you like to go for a ride on my bike?" Khriss shows his stained yellow teeth and he glares at her like he was offering her the best deal ever. "We'd even take your kid along."

"Awwright! I've got my own car," Kheyla snarls.

A sudden menacing growl followed by deafening barking startles the child.

"Look who's here," Khriss says. "We'll take the dog along too." He laughs.

The fox terrier races out of the backyard, scampering along the eastern wall of the house. The animal races to Thistle, wags its tail and leaps up to sniff his crotch.

"Kuster! Down. General." Thistle ruffles the dog's fur. He tickles the terrier's right ear. "Am I ever glad to see you, Kus! Thought I'd lost you. I was afraid I'd never see you again when I left you waiting outside the store. But I knew you wouldn't let me down."

A siren shrieks in the distance. "What now?" Khriss stares down the road and he glances at his bike.

Thistle bends to talk to his dog. "Listen, boy. You keep the cops and their sniffing friend busy as I clean up the crop at back. Don't mind, do you?" He pats the animal's head and then hurries to the back of the house to work in the garden.

A blue striped cruiser brakes in front of the house. Two cops jump out with a police dog. They walk around the Plymouth. The shorter one glances at the child who sucks his thumb on his mother's lap.

"Is this your car?" The shorter cop's moustache quivers like a fly under his nose. Kheyla nods.

Karyn scowls, but the constables ignore her. She heads back to the house as Khriss remains near his bike. Both policemen march along the path leading to the back where the soil in the small patch of garden is black and humid as if it had just been turned over. The dark-haired dog paws at a few lumps of dirt and sniffs the ground, but finds nothing. Nobody could prove that Mary Jean had been transplanted, like a lover looking for a better life.

The officers knock at the front door. Karyn lets them in. Kuster sniffs around the tail of the growling police dog.

"Stop that, Kuster," Karyn says. "Leave the guests be."

She finds a bone-shaped biscuit for each of the two animals that settle down, gnawing next to each other.

"Rhena!" the moustache calls out, tugging at the leash. "Don't be so greedy." But the dog pulls back and continues to chew. "What's the matter? You in love or something?" The officer wraps the leash tight around his fist, but the animal doesn't budge.

The other constable paces around the living room. He searches for clues among the empty beer bottles. The cop looks puzzled. "Nothing here."

"Rhena! Let's go. Don't chew that carpet."

Both cops strut outside. They walk to their cruiser with their dog still whining and pulling at the leash.

Thistle wipes his hands on his jeans. Before the police could find out what had been growing in the backyard, he had pulled out the marijuana plants. He squeezed them together tight into a basket fastened to the back seat of his brother's motorcycle.

"Drive down to Thistle Creek," he said to Khriss who roared away with his cargo.

Karyn looks out the window. She watches the Plymouth pull away. The cruiser is still parked in front of the house.

"Come here, Thistle. Look. My car's gone."

"Yeah! Don't worry about that. The cops will go away soon. We have a lot to do. A lot of catching up."

She nods. His mouth is warm on her skin and his tongue feels hot searching for hers. Wet. Kind of grating. His bristles scrape against her neck, but she doesn't mind.

The siren of the cruiser screams outside for a moment and Karyn doesn't care. She knows Thistle won't leave her.

"Guess, you have to stick around, Thistle," she says. "Can't live without me for long."

"Neither can you stay without me." He hugs her and she scratches the back of his neck.

"Let's take Kuster for a hike down to Thistle Creek."

He watches her walk the dog along the lonely path down to Thistle Creek. It's quiet. Hot. Maybe Karyn will even go skinny-dipping before the day is over.

THE SUMMER UNIFORM

A lead sky and a light drizzle. It was still my birthday and I was looking forward to the presents. My mother always prepared rows of red and yellow apples on a cookie tray for my birthday. She washed the fruits and cut out their cores. She lined up the apples neatly. I couldn't take my eyes off the red, shiny globes. They looked like the gold and red decorations that would soon hang from the green pine tree standing in the window of the grocery store on main street. My mother would let me sprinkle a pinch of icing sugar as white as snow on top of the unpeeled apples. She might add a touch of cinnamon before she would slide the tray inside the warm oven. The spicy fragrance of baked apples would spread through the kitchen and the living room. I would taste the glazed fruit. Sweet like a candy apple. My birthday wouldn't be the same without the sugary treat. But that was a very bad year for fruit trees. A killer frost hit the apple orchard. It didn't stop at that. A crust of ice, frothy white like spit, coated plums, peaches and pear trees. The grapes did not survive. My father lost his job as a fruit picker and to make things worse my baby brother caught chicken pox.

I remember how I felt when I came home from school that day. My coat was wet from the drizzle and felt as heavy as lead, yet I didn't even take it off. I ran into the kitchen.

No fruit on the counter top. Not a single apple. The shelves in the cupboards were bare. There was no food left except for a few crusts of old *pagnotta* bread. Hunger pangs chewed at my stomach.

My mother stood as a silent shadow by the window. When I glanced at her, she bowed her head. Nothing on the cookie tray. Her hair was combed straight back and she didn't wear her feisty silk blouse with bold yellow sunflowers for my special day.

Early that same morning, my father had left the house, slamming the front door shut. He went out, looking for work. Any kind of work. He believed he could find a job in construction, but jobs were scarce and we didn't know if he would have any luck.

In the kitchen, my mother stared at me shoving the cupboard doors closed. Bang. She joined her hands together and rolled her eyes upward as if she were praying.

My coat was getting heavier. I slipped my arms out of the sleeves, took my coat off and placed my books on my desk. Usually, I didn't mind doing my homework, but this was a special day. It was my birthday after all. I was hungry and wanted to eat my sugar-coated apples.

I glanced at my doll, Maddie, sitting at the foot of my bed in her pink flower print dress. She looked too comfortable to be disturbed and I didn't want to pick her up. As I tapped Maddie's shoulders lightly to puff up her sleeves and I straightened the red ribbon at her waist, I wished I could have a pet to share with my family. But my parents would not let me. We couldn't afford that.

Maddie's round, rosy cheeks reminded me of my little brother, Sandro, who was just three months old. Sandro started to cry in the bedroom.

My mother warmed up some milk in the bottle and

brought it into the bedroom to feed my baby brother. She slid the rubber nipple between his tiny pursed lips. With his chubby little hands, my baby brother grabbed the bottle. He began sucking and gurgling, but he quickly lost interest. His small mouth let go of the nipple. He pushed the bottle away until he could kick it with his little foot. The bottle rolled down to the other side of his crib. He closed his eyes and his eyelids quivered. He was making wheezing sounds as he breathed. Small blisters and tiny red spots dotted his face and neck. His forehead felt burning hot. He was running a high fever.

My mother tried to make him swallow a baby Aspirin to get the fever down. His small face turned violet as he clenched his little fists. He spat the Aspirin out and cried louder, as if to let us know we weren't doing the right thing. We had no money to buy any antibiotics for him and we were waiting for my father to return with some news.

When we heard a loud knock later on that afternoon, both my mother and I rushed to open the door. It was Marina, our shapely neighbour, who brought over a gold-coloured focaccia braided as a thick wreath encrusted with candied red cherries and orange rinds. The creamy-white handkerchief wrapped around her head made her look like a busy chef at work. Marina wore the butter-yellow popcorn sweater my mother had knit for her because we were short of money and she saved some day-old bread loaves for us at the bakery. Two purple cyclamens with cinnamon pistils bloomed at her earlobes. They were the fancy earrings her boyfriend Dario enjoyed nuzzling while hugging her in the doorway after work.

Marina lived with her aunt across the street from us. She would leave in the morning to go to the bakery where she mixed flour and stretched dough for tasty cinnamon twisters, or hot cross buns. Dario would walk her home in the evening. The two lovers embraced and squeezed each other as they stood in the shadow of the doorway. Marina would put her head on his shoulder and he would nibble at her earrings as if they were roasted mallows.

Everyone in the village expected them to get married, but her aunt wouldn't hear of it. Aunt Bianchina would yell, "Get back in the house, Marina! Right now." Marina would climb up the stairway and Dario would wait on the street below until the light went on in her room.

The trouble started when he showed up in his khaki uniform one day when he was called to serve in the army. Since childhood, Bianchina was scared of soldiers. They had raped her during the last war. They stuffed her into a flour sack and dragged her around for days until the Allies dropped a bomb during an air raid. It exploded, killing her tormentors, destroying their jeep and throwing her fifteen metres away in the ditch. Her parents had died in an ambush and only her older sister survived.

Marina loved Dario's new summer uniform. But her aunt chased him away with her broom when she saw him.

"Can't marry a soldier. He's got a gun to shoot people. He'll kill you. Look at his hands. Cut and bruised as if he'd fought a many-headed monster. He will hurt you. He works even on Sunday with his damn shotgun and hand grenades instead of going to church. Pull yourself together, girl." A door would slam shut and several thuds followed.

"No. Aunt. No." Marina would weep. "There's no war now. He won't kill anyone."

"Hell! Don't push me too far. I know what soldiers are like. Silly girl. I wanted to help your mother. But she got in trouble with a sergeant. She died giving birth. My own sister. You killed her. I had to raise you. Now, you turn against me. Ready to bite me, like a viper." Aunt Bianchina would cough. "At this rate you'll kill me too. Because of that no-good-bum of yours. Dario's a soldier. A socialist. Hard-boiled, hot-headed loafer stuck out too far at the left. Too far gone to be straightened out. Wanted to run for the party, joining the Communists, worse than Fascists," her aunt shrieked. "How can you do this to me? My own flesh and blood." She would pick up her broom and several loud bangs echoed throughout the house.

"No!" Marina would go to work next morning, nursing a black eye swollen shut. She would wear layers of makeup to cover the bruises on her cheeks and brow. She would never admit she had trouble at home.

Marina stared at us that afternoon, holding the golden foccacia. "It's Sarah's birthday and I baked this focaccia. Here." Marina handed the honey-gold wreath over to my mother. "Try a slice. Still warm from the oven."

With both hands, my mother took the sweet focaccia. "Shouldn't have done so much work for us."

Marina winked at me. "And this is also for you, Sarah!" She gave me a tiny box wrapped in spice-coloured paper.

"For me?" I tugged at the golden bow as if it would yield the most delicious secret in the world. I was hoping it would be a pair of cinnamon earrings like hers. I tore off the paper, opened the box and took out a raisin necklace with an almond pendant. I cradled the pendant in my cupped hands. "Wow!" It was an ivory cameo carved against the dark hues of the burnt brown skin of the almond.

Marina nodded. "I've chiseled in your profile. Thought you might like it."

I slid the raisin necklace over my head, but it caught my hair and dangled from my right ear. I tugged at the almond charm. "It's my new earring."

"A fancy edible earring." Marina flashed a smile showing a row of even white teeth. "It frames part of your thin face. Too thin. You need to eat some focaccia."

I stared at the golden wreath. Its fruity scent was too much for me and my empty stomach. I stretched out my middle finger and touched the sugary crust. I licked my fingertip.

"Wait, Sarah!" My mother placed the round focaccia on the kitchen table. The sweet fragrance wafted in waves and made me swallow some saliva. I could almost taste the spongy texture of the focaccia, as if I'd taken a bite. My mother gave me the first slice. "Let's try it."

I tasted the honey-coated crust. It melted in my mouth. I ate the almond slivers on top. A bit hard to chew, but I could still swallow them. My tongue lapped at a glossy red cherry, the size of a small tomato.

Marina watched me, then she turned to my mother. "I have something for your baby." She fumbled in the pocket of her turquoise skirt until she pulled out a green glass jar filled with dried herbs, yellow wrinkled petals and pistils crushed into tiny bits, small as pinheads.

"What is it?"

"Chamomile. They look like daisies."

"I'll give him a bit. I'd try anything." My mother sighed. "He is running a fever."

"Let him drink chamomile mixed with boiled water and warm milk. It will lower his fever and make him sleep," Marina said. "You can sponge his little head and body with a damp towel at room temperature. He needs to breathe fresh air. He'll get rid of the chicken pox."

My mother took the tiny jar. She shook it, as if it were a kaleidoscope of green leaves, yellow pistils and frazzled petals shaping different, exotic flowers. Baby Sandro began to cry in his crib. My mother waved the chamomile jar in the air and rushed into the bedroom to pick up my little brother. She cuddled him in her arms.

Marina walked back through the hallway and reached for the brass doorknob at the entrance. She turned the metal knob and unlocked the door. As she stepped outside, a big cinnamon-coloured cat raced inside the house. A furry ball of sugar and spice.

"Catch it if you can," Marina said to me. "It's all yours." She turned around, crossed the street and disappeared in her doorway.

I nodded. I couldn't believe my eyes.

Hypnotized, I glanced at the fuzzy ball of fur, a blur of cinnamon and ocher. The feline scrambled around the legs of the coffee table and sniffed the paisley padded seat of the high-back chair. The cat clawed the air and scampered to hide under the burnt-orange chesterfield in the living room.

In the dark bedroom, the baby still sobbed. My mother cradled him in her arms, placed him back in his crib and tucked his blue-rimmed blanket under his chin. She left the room and tiptoed to the front door to make sure it was shut. She hurried into the kitchen and boiled a cup of water to prepare some chamomile tea.

The cinnamon-coloured cat hissed at me in the living room. Its white-striped whiskers shivered under the velvet collar of the chesterfield. Smothering a giggle in my throat, I stretched out my right arm. Its tail was coiling around one of the wooden legs of the chesterfield and I felt the soft cinnamon fur brush against my hand.

I smiled. "Sien-Sien!" I called him, peering under the chesterfield. But at that moment, a blood-curdling shriek pierced the air.

"Hoooowwwl!"

I gasped. I did not know what went wrong. The echo of the nerve-wracking scream lingered in the air.

"My baby!" my mother cried out and scurried back into the bedroom.

Her face as white as a bed sheet, my mother stood by the baby's crib. Her lips trembled as she handed the refilled bottle to my little brother who grabbed it and started to suck the warm milk mixed with chamomile tea. He kept on gulping the amber drink until he fell asleep still sucking.

A pink, healthy tint slowly returned to his cheeks and his breathing became normal. My mother touched his forehead. "Doesn't feel too hot anymore. Guess the chamomile Marina gave us works." She waved to me. "Your little brother drank his milk. Now, he looks better. He's a fighter and wants to get rid of the chicken pox." She straightened the blue trimmed blanket and pulled it up to his chin. "Did you hear that terrible scream? I was scared. Thought something awful happened to my little Sandro. Sounded dreadful." She glowered at me.

I bowed my head. I didn't want to let her know I had pulled the cat's tail. Felt bad about that. I was not sure how she would treat the unexpected visitor. She might get mad at me, or even worse, at my new pet. I strolled back into the living room and bent over to look under the chesterfield.

"Sien-Sien," I murmured. "It's not safe to come out yet. Wait right there. Don't move!"

Sien-Sien was curled up, nested near the wall. I just wished to pick up the cinnamon cat and cuddle him in my arms. I'd take care of my new pet. I'd always wanted a fuzzy cinnamon cat like that to pet and pamper. This was my chance. My birthday gift. Sien-Sien had chosen our home to visit and I was sure my furry pet would enjoy staying with us. Sien-Sien and I could get along very well.

My mother put on her apron. She grasped the handle of the broom in the storage closet near the kitchen.

"What's that on the floor? Mud? Grass? Did you bring dirt in?" She started sweeping the red-tiled floor. She open-ed the front door.

Sien-Sien dashed across the living room and raced through the hall. Silent as a mouse, my cat slipped out of the house before I could even touch it and pet it again.

"Noo. Nooo!" I broke into sobs. I ran out. I searched outside and raced across the street. "Sien-Sien!" I yelled until I was hoarse. I looked up and down main street. Sien-Sien was nowhere in sight.

My father was walking home when he found me. He wiped the tears from my face, took my hand and brought me back inside the house.

He shared the news with us that evening. He had met Marina's boyfriend, Dario, who was in charge of an im-portant construction project nearby. He learned the con-struction trade when he joined the army. Now, they were building a large grocery store up the block and Dario told my father to apply for a job as a bricklayer. My father started right away to work on the construction site. He laboured on the site for a few hours that afternoon, earning much-needed cash to feed his family.

He bought some milk, grissini and red apples to cel-ebrate my birthday. We baked one fruit for each one of us, including my little brother who tasted some of the sweet flesh of the sugar-coated apple and didn't spit it out.

I believe that was one of the best birthdays I ever had, although I could not avoid the gnawing longing for my furry cinnamon cat. I remember how often I looked out of the window to see if I could find Sien-Sien stalking a mouse, or darting across the wide street. But I could only see Dario chewing at Marina's cyclamen earrings.

Next day at dusk, I noticed Sien-Sien racing along the road. The cinnamon cat was scampering past the doorway where Marina and her boyfriend hugged each other. I drew the heavy curtains, but couldn't stop watching Sien-Sien through the small opening left in the middle.

Marina's aunt suddenly appeared in the doorway. She lifted her broom high above her head and hit her niece. Marina crumpled to the ground and Dario picked her up and held her in his arms. She was bleeding from a gash near her temple and blood spurted out staining his uniform.

My mother caught me peeking through the curtains. "What are you looking at?" She shoved me against the wall. "Stay away from this window. Can't spy on the neighbours." She glanced outside. "Maybe we should call the parish priest. Somebody." She took a deep breath, then cradled her head in her hands as if she didn't want to face another problem.

Three days later, Marina returned home from the hospital. She had regained consciousness at the emergency. But she didn't know what happened to her. She went back to work at the bakery. Dario moved away and now lives in another village.

Marina doesn't wear her earrings with cyclamens and cinnamon pistils anymore. Maybe she lost them when her aunt attacked her with the broom. Every time she walks down the street, Marina glances around as if she is looking for what she has lost.

I'm still searching for my cat and maybe I'll find Sien-Sien one day. I miss that little ball of fur. If I could cradle my pet in my arms, I'd stroll along main street. I wouldn't mind going over to the bakery and cheering up Marina.

My Tough Teeth

Early this morning, I went to see a new dentist. Every time I need a checkup, I change dentists. I don't have to say why. I am sure everyone understands me. Wearing my new white dress didn't help as much as I'd thought. I still don't like to go to the dentist, just as I don't enjoy to bring my sister's kids to the zoo. They run around as if they are in their natural habitat, but I don't feel at home when I visit the dentist.

Before I was allowed to sit on THE CHAIR, I had to fill in a long sheet of paper with my whole medical history. I guess he wanted to make sure I didn't suffer from heart disease, diabetes or AIDS before he checked my teeth. Maybe, the new dentist wanted to find out whether I could withstand the sharpest of drills. I was worried. He probably was eager to show off the skills he had acquired at school. I didn't relish the idea of becoming a guinea pig.

Trapped in his chair, I felt tied down and I couldn't move. I couldn't talk. He didn't bother freezing my mouth and I tried to calm down. *I sure hope he likes his work*, I thought. *After all, he has to practice on somebody. Why not on me? Give him a chance.*

I don't know why at a time like this he glanced at me and asked, "Are you comfortable, Ms. Welster?"

I had no other choice but to nod approval as if I sat on

top of the world. He appeared rather pleased. The faint sound of a keyboard playing a popular tune on the radio spread through the air and he brandished an awful instrument that sported a long metal hook approaching my stretched wide-open mouth. I wished I could have told him I had changed my mind. I wanted to leave. It was too late.

Poking my gums without pity, he seemed as fierce as a cold-blooded pirate sporting his iron pick searching for a hidden treasure. He could wave his flag with skull and bones before attacking my teeth. I was about to scream and tell him I had no gold in my teeth and he could stop poking around in there. But how could I say anything with his fist in my mouth?

The metal hook clinked against my top canines and I clenched my fists. I always thought my teeth were just fine for me and he should know better than fishing for cavities in my mouth. Even my friends agree they don't make teeth as good as they used to. Fixing teeth is cheaper now. They drill, put in a cheap filling and charge as if it's worth more than your own tooth.

The dentist stared at me as if he wanted to give me bad news. He twitched his bushy eyebrows and grinned, showing off a bluish row of front teeth as sharp as eagle claws. "What kind of work do you do?"

That was what I should have asked him. I didn't expect to face that kind of question, especially when he was busy working on my teeth. How could I answer with that metal hook scraping and hitting my lower molars? That was too much. I wasn't going to let him know I write, or he might have more fun with his drill than I could ever have with my computer. Wait a minute. You never know. Maybe he *understands* everything about computers. I would have to be careful. I wouldn't want him to start out working on the wrong tooth.

"Hah! Let me guess . . . You're in real estate!" he exclaimed with his toothy grin. "That's a hard job these days. Jobs are scarce. Prices are climbing up to the sky. Most people think they're buying a skyscraper instead of a mere two-storey house for their families."

He walked to the front of THE CHAIR where I sat quietly. Drawing his eyebrows together, he continued to stare at me with a quizzical look on his face. Maybe he expected me to say something. *I can't go very far if I lie*, I thought. *I have to tell him the truth.*

"I . . . I type," I mumbled. What else could I say with the metal hook still poking around my gums?

"You're a secretary, I see!" He sighed and stuck his fist in my mouth again. "What a perfect job for a woman who wants to be independent! I bet you began typing when you decided to be your own boss. You wanted to be on your own, right?" He withdrew his hooked instrument for a moment and balanced himself on one foot.

Baring my teeth, I glared at him. I have seen dogs bare their fangs to scare the enemy. I was doing the same. I had to keep my mouth stretched wide open for him to poke into. I couldn't disappoint my new dentist. In some way, I wished to impress him. I'd like him to think I'm much better than I am in reality. *Maybe he will appreciate my teeth too*, I thought. Of course, I must admit I can appreciate my teeth even more than he ever will. I can say they are tough and do their job well for me.

As he continued poking my gums around my incisors, he tightened the muscles of his grim face. "Secretaries are hard-working people. Strong. Tough-skinned. People think they can work faster with computers these days. But if we can tell a secretary to do better, how can we ask that kind of question to a computer?"

That's it, I thought. *I should do better. At least, that's what everyone tells me. Perhaps, I'll switch jobs. I'll become a secretary. Or a receptionist. Why not give it a try? I'll have a better chance to make it. Many of my friends work in offices and earn good salaries. I'm sure all the secretaries I know are better off than I am.*

The dentist picked up another instrument. A bigger hook. *What am I waiting for? This might just be the right moment to stop him before he starts fishing inside my mouth again.*

With a timid smile, I glanced at the dentist. "Are you looking for a new secretary by any chance? Or hiring a receptionist?"

"No, not with all the computer equipment we have available now. We feed in some data and the computer spits out all the figures we want." He shoved the huge metal hook in my mouth. It became stuck, wedged between the last two molars on my lower jaw. "What do we have here?"

The droopy-eyed receptionist walked in. She wore pink lipstick and metallic blue eye shadow. She stretched her long neck to reach the dentist's ear. "The vet's on the telephone," she murmured. "Wants to let you know . . . ."

"How is Hairy doing?" The dentist waved the huge hook in the air and I didn't mind at all seeing it *out* of my mouth.

"Hairy had his booster shots and also a vaccine against rabies."

"Go on."

"Might need a back tooth pulled out."

The dentist's face crimsoned. "I can find that out easily. It's my job." He looked around as if he didn't know how to make himself understood. "I'll have to pick up Hairy later, in the afternoon." He shrugged.

The receptionist bowed her head. "Needs some work on his teeth."

"How could the vet say such a thing? Should know better than that," he hissed.

"The vet thinks you shouldn't be working on your own pet. It's too emotional." The girl sighed.

"Draining."

"Too close to you."

The dentist shook his head. "My pug needs the best of care. The kind only I can give." He didn't seem so fierce anymore. He dropped his instrument onto a tray, as if he was tired and felt beat doing such a tough job on my teeth.

The slim receptionist lowered her eyelids, nodding like she understood what he didn't say. Her starched uniform swished as she left the room.

The dentist turned to me. "You're doing well, Ms. Welster. No cavities. You've got tough teeth. It will just take a minute to add up your bill, don't worry." He peeled off his thin rubber gloves and wiped his hands with a white linen towel. He pressed down a lever with the right foot and lowered THE CHAIR.

On my way out, I stopped at the receptionist's desk. A computer keyboard clicked and the girl looked at me with her moist blue eyes. She stabbed some of the grey keys on the keyboard and the monitor flashed several numbers, amber and gold like capped teeth. The printer hummed, crackled and spewed out a long tongue of pale yellow paper. It was like a pirate flag flying a last salute. It could have been worse.

The receptionist turned to me and handed me the bill. Her teeth shone white, matching her starched uniform. I thought she might have had them painted with high-gloss enamel.

I wrote a cheque and gave it to her. She took it, slid it through a slot in the cash register and then stamped it with blue ink. She didn't even ask my ID and I left in a hurry.

Now, I'm glad to be back at my computer. It's a good feeling and I don't mind some peace and quiet. I know I can work much faster and I'll become much better. It won't take me long to improve my skills if I stop taking my sister's kids to the zoo.

I think I'll have to change my style, my *modus vivendi*, just like I switch dentists.

CAGED

Children, bundled up with scarves and wool mittens, were walking to school that cool autumn morning. In ankle-length skirts, a few women were heading for the Farmers' Market to buy ripe saffron persimmons, tufted carrots, red potatoes and purple onions. Whistling, a skinny delivery boy rode his bike, its wicker basket filled with freshly baked bread loaves peeking out of brown paper bags like baseball bats. He let go of his handlebars and bounced over the cobblestones to show off until he almost fell. But he kept on pedaling and whistling.

A few vehicles screeched to a halt as the light turned orange at the intersection leading to the cobbled square where the pinnacled cathedral stood milky white, like a lighthouse sending out a beam combing the area for lost ships. It turned red and brakes squealed, but a khaki truck skidded past, its tires scraping the bottom of pot holes and mud puddles.

Boom! Crash! The ground shook as if a hand grenade had exploded in the middle of the street. One of the front wheels of the truck grated against the curb and jumped over the sidewalk. It scrubbed a slab of concrete steps. The bumper hit a biker who tumbled off his bike and smashed his leg against a metre-high stone protecting the corner walls of a meat delicatessen. The impact shattered the glass window of the shop, spraying the customers with debris. Glass slivers and shards rained onto the sidewalk. Metal splinters shot out like shrapnel and dug into the wall. The smell of burnt rubber lingered in the air as the truck roared spewing fumes from the exhaust. The broad shouldered driver veered to the left and sped away on the cobblestones.

A crumpled bike lay abandoned on the side of the road, its metal frame bent and folded like an accordion. The handlebars sat chewed and twisted like a wire hanger. Curled into a fetal position on the sidewalk, the wounded biker moaned, his left foot sticking out at an odd angle from underneath a black cassock smeared with blood.

Dark-clad women stood in shock among the rubble. My grandmother wiped some blood from the cut on her forehead and darted over broken glass to help the biker.

"Who got hurt?" a woman wondered, waving her bleeding hand.

"Poor man," a black-veiled woman echoed. "The truck raced away in a hurry, but won't get anywhere."

"It's Father Rico!" My grandmother bent over him.

"Nooo," the veiled woman wailed. "God help us!" She turned away. "It's an omen. Something awful is going to happen to us." She elbowed my grandmother's ribs as the crowd closed in around the wounded biker.

"Let me see if we can help him," my grandmother said.

"Don't want to see him hurt bad." The woman pulled her black veil over her eyes and face. "Can't stand the sight of blood." Her chest heaved as she sobbed.

"Can't let him bleed to death under our own eyes. On the street. He's wounded. Maimed." My grandmother took off her black shawl, folded it and slipped it under Father Rico's head, and his eyelids shuddered. "All we need now is something to tie around his leg and stop the bleeding."

Unmoving, the priest lay curled up on the cold concrete of the sidewalk. Red rivulets trickled down from his
nostrils to his chin. His lips moved slightly, but no sound
came out of his mouth. Blood oozed from the left leg bent
at an awkward angle.

My grandmother went down on her knees. Her head
bowed, she took his pulse. He opened his eyes, staring past
her, as if he had never seen her before. His shoulders shook
as he coughed and wheezed. He had a hard time breathing.

"So cold," he whispered. "I'm very cold." His teeth were
chattering as he glanced at my grandmother.

She took off her charcoal sweater and covered the
priest. "How's that?"

"God sent you to me! You remind me of Maura. *Pater
Noster*." He twisted his torso to one side and he tried to
prop himself up onto his elbow. "Oowww!" He dropped
down again, lying on the cold sidewalk.

"Take it easy, Father Rico." With a white handkerchief,
my grandmother wiped some sweat off the priest's haggard
face.

"My leg hurts." He took a deep breath. The gash in his
thigh reached down to the bone.

"We must stop the bleeding." My grandmother ripped
the long leather strap from her purse and wrapped it tight
around the priest's thigh. The heavy bleeding became only a
trickle.

"Ouch, this pain is unbearable!" he complained, but
didn't draw back from my grandmother's firm hands.

"Must be courageous. Don't mean to hurt you."

"My leg burns like it's on fire."

"Have to tighten the strap like a tourniquet around
your leg. You'll get better soon," my grandmother said as if
she knew everything about medicine. She read widely to

keep up with new medical discoveries. She learned to give herself injections of vitamin B12 for her anemia. A caring person, she wanted to be able to treat the wounded after air raids. You'd never know how things may turn out.

"The Lord won't forget what you're doing for me." The priest grimaced. "Neither will I."

The black-clad women stood around watching. Kids didn't dare approach too closely. They stood at a distance, their mouth open. Only the delivery boy picked up the broken bike and leaned the twisted wreak against the wall.

My grandmother glanced around. "Did someone call an ambulance?"

"Think so," replied the woman who hid most of her face behind the black veil, but couldn't take her eyes off the priest. "The delivery boy called from the delicatessen." She gestured toward the skinny boy who stared at the priest as if he wished to help him out but didn't know how.

"Aren't the medics coming soon?" The woman with bleeding hands pointed to the youth.

The gaunt-faced boy nodded. "Yeah!" He lowered his chin to his chest. His T-shirt slipped from his nape to uncover the iron chain and cross he wore around his neck. He kneeled beside the injured priest and strengthened the tourniquet on his leg by using his bike's pump to keep it taut. "Is this better?"

Father Rico stared at the boy's chain and grimaced. "Are you serving Mass this Sunday?" he whispered to the boy who sucked in a corner of his lips. The priest stretched out his arm to bless him, but shut his eyes as if he were blinded by a sudden light and lost consciousness.

A siren howled closer. An ambulance was rushing to the scene. The white vehicle with a red cross painted on the sides and doors, jolted to a halt near the curb. Two paramedics in lime green uniforms jumped down. They slipped a stretcher out of the rear of the ambulance and they placed it next to Father Rico, still motionless on the sidewalk. As the two medics were about to slide the priest onto the stretcher, a police cruiser drove up, its bright red light flashing on top of the roof. A swarthy constable got off and stomped to where the priest lay. The officer pushed back his blue visor cap and stared at the women standing in a circle around Father Rico.

"Did anybody witness this accident?" the constable asked in a deep throaty voice. He sounded hoarse as if he had been screaming and still nobody would listen to him. No one replied. No one moved. His eyes watched the black veil swell, floating in the wind, as a hand quickly grasped it. "You want to tell me something?"

"Who would do this to our parish priest? To a holy man? Why didn't that hit-and-run truck stop?" The black veil was shaking. "Must be a monster. The worst trucker ever. Couldn't see what he was doing."

"What kind of truck was he driving?" The constable frowned.

"A khaki truck."

"An army truck?" The constable started taking notes.

"Guess so." The woman tugged at her veil and wrapped it tighter around her head as if she needed protection.

"Can you describe the driver?"

"Tough-looking. A balding head. Buttoned-up shirt, but a clump of black hair grew out of the collar to cover his throat. A werewolf. Hope he doesn't get us all in trouble."

"Anybody see him before?" asked the serious constable, glancing around to pick up what wasn't yet said.

"Just a minute." My grandmother touched her forehead as if to remember. She patted her cut from the glass shard.

The blood had started to coagulate. "I think I've seen him before. Must be a top dog. He had a bristly moustache growing like a black cockroach under his nose."

"Some crazy fellow." The black veil quivered. A dark butterfly. "Wouldn't want to meet him on the street at night. Gives me the creeps."

"The priest couldn't have any enemies, could he?" The officer watched the bystanders with apprehension.

"Don't think so." The wind blew harder on the veil and the woman stretched out her arm to stop it from flying away again. "He's a saint."

The medics were sliding Father Rico onto their long canvas stretcher. The policeman glared at the black-clad women, like he didn't believe he could get the information he needed to arrest the trucker and to charge him with criminal negligence.

"Did anyone see the license plate of that vehicle?" The policeman wasn't going to give up gathering clues leading to the arrest of the driver.

"Couldn't notice the numbers." My grandmother looked down at her feet. "The back plate was caked with mud. And the driver sped away faster than the devil."

"Hope he goes to hell!" the woman with bloody hands shouted. "To hell!"

The priest's eyelids trembled. He squinted as if he were blinded by the day's light. "Don't say that," he scolded the woman. "God is testing all of us. We have to accept what's in store for us. Whether we like it or not."

"Look at what that crazy trucker did to you." The other woman pushed back her black veil from a plump face. Two moles were welded together on her chin. "Is it fair?"

"I forgive him," the priest sighed, reaching for his leg with both hands.

"What did he look like?" With a sudden glow of hope in his eyes, the policeman bent over the priest.

"I'm not sure. His face looked kind of familiar. Don't know if he is an old acquaintance of mine or not. Maybe I saw him in a dream. I forgive him whoever he is."

"And you'd turn the other cheek, huh?" The black veil flipped back as the woman folded it over her shoulders.

"I wouldn't." The priest grimaced as the medics covered him with a grey blanket and tucked it under his chin. They were going to lift the stretcher. "Wouldn't want to get my other leg broken." Don Rico still had the sense of humour he would always need for his sermons at Mass on Sunday.

Shoving back the blue cap on his head, the constable exposed his brush cut. He motioned to the medics. "Take care of this good soul."

The heavier-set medic nodded. With his partner, he carried Father Rico to the rear of the ambulance. They slid the stretcher inside and slammed the back doors shut. Both medics got in. The ambulance drove away, its siren shrieking as if pleading for help.

Scowling, the officer stared at the remaining twisted metal pieces of the bike scattered on the road like bullet shells. He cordoned off the area.

"We might find some chips of paint from the runaway vehicle," the constable said. He crouched to examine the tangled mess of broken glass from the shattered store window. "Somebody must have witnessed this accident. What about the person who called for an ambulance?"

The delivery boy, who had phoned earlier from the store, was nowhere to be found. He had disappeared with his bike. The few distraught women left at the scene pointed to my grandmother.

"She saw the accident," they said in unison.

The constable turned to face my grandmother with a strict expression. "You did?"

"Didn't see much," my grandmother said. "A trucker rushed through the intersection as the light turned red. He bounced onto the sidewalk. I tried to take a look at him, but he sped up towards me."

"The coward!" The constable wrote down a few notes.

"Spotted Don Rico halting at the light," my grandmother went on. "He was about to place his foot on the metre-high rock in the corner by *Spinacci Delicatessen*. A loud crash. The window of the shop shattered and Don Rico went flying. Next thing I know, he's on the ground. In a pool of blood."

The officer scanned the faces of the bystanders who stood silent. Some of them were nodding. He slipped his notepad into his pocket.

"Something real bad is going to happen. I know." The short woman stretched out her bloody hands, reaching out to the lead sky as if looking for a sort of reassurance from heaven. "Can feel it in my blood. In my bones."

"When a good man is hit, it's never going to be the same." The constable gathered a few twisted fragments of metal.

The woman wrapped in her black veil gestured at the bottleneck. "That's a bad intersection leading to the cobbled square where the *Duomo* and the red brick Ducal Palace still stand after the bombings. Too many army trucks race by. Some of them shake the *Duomo* as they rattle over the cobblestones. Why don't they widen the road to avoid accidents?"

"They don't want to demolish the historical buildings framing the square," the constable replied.

The black veil shivered. "It's too bad. They don't need

those army trucks. If all they can do is run over a priest, what good are they for?"

The constable adjusted his blue crested cap on his head. "One sheep has strayed from the flock. But they are not all that bad."

Bowing their heads, the women sighed.

Everyone in town knew that Father Rico fought his own personal battles. He preached against the war and he did what he could to save many people. He lived with modest means in the rectory beside the cathedral and he would look after the poor with open arms. He always kept a pot of chicken soup on his stove. At noon, hungry people lined up at his door and Rico would serve them bowls of hot soup. He would never turn anyone away.

As he used to do each day after the eight o'clock Mass, Don Rico walked out of the sacristy that crisp autumn morning. He wore his black cassock, its hem sweeping his thin-soled leather sandals. He tucked the sides like two big drapes under his belt and hopped onto his shiny bike. Rico was going in the direction of *Via Giustiziati* and pedaled past the brick Ducal Palace dominating the wide *Sordello Square*. Cars rattled over the rough cobblestones of the square. It was the beginning of the morning rush hour and several farmers were heading for the market with their carts full of produce. Women in long cotton smocks would set up their wooden stands in the Square of the Herbs, not far from the fountain where a naked angel sprinkled water gushing out of his trumpet. The farmers' wives would arrange crispy lettuce and leafy-green cabbages into potbellied crates. Some of them would pile up wrinkled red tomatoes on sagging wooden boards which served as shelves and they kept the rare eggplants and celery stalks under their display table for their best customers. The cheese vendor set up his kiosk and got ready for customers like Father Rico who would haggle for *pecorino* or goat cheese.

Slim and fit like a soccer player, Father Rico would often go fishing in the nearby Lake Superior. But he would hook only catfish and he would throw his catch back into the lake. He worked hard in the garden behind the cathedral to grow vegetables for the hungry and he would perspire under the hot summer sun. Some skin would peel off his stubby nose and his tanned fingers would dig into black dirt as if they were roots searching for nourishment.

In the fall, he would harvest beets, string beans, carrots, spinach, potatoes, tomatoes and peas.

"God will let me grow enough green beans, *fagioli,* to feed the whole congregation," he would often say. "We need all we can get these days, God knows."

Don Rico would always head for the newsstand near the southern corner of the grey stone police station. He tossed some coins for the daily Gazette as the street vendor went on screaming to attract customers. The lines on the priest's brow deepened as he read the local news and his sturdy jaw tightened as if he were a sprinter about to start the most important race of his life.

That morning, he frowned at the sudden yelling and commotion on the other side of the square. Two tousled-haired boys groaned, rolling over the dirty cobblestones. The two kids punched, kicked and bit each other, locked into a fist fight. Father Rico rushed past the curious crowd gathering around the wrestlers. He clenched his jaw, put two fingers into his mouth and whistled as if he were halting traffic. The two kids fought harder.

A dog shot out of a dark doorway nearby. It was the black and brown-haired mongrel everyone spoiled.

"Fido!" Father Rico yelled and the animal ran to sniff around his feet. "There! You tell them, doggie." Fido barked at the two kids who sprang up. The boys took turns scratching behind the ears of the mongrel. The dog wagged its tail and watched the priest fumble in his pocket for a small brown paper bag. He took out a bone and threw it to Fido. As if it had not eaten for months, the animal began to gnaw at the bone.

"Can we play soccer with you next week, Padre?" The kids tugged at the priest's sleeve. They both had scrapes dotting their noses like freckles and their shirts were torn, but they looked settled down by now like they both had just won a wrestling match.

Father Rico nodded to them, and they strolled away talking, grinning at each other.

The priest crossed the cobbled square and stared at the rifle-toting *carabinieri* standing on guard beside the studded metal door of the police station. The two *carabinieri* scowled, clicked the heels of their black boots and stuck out their chests and chins, saluting the row of spindly chestnut trees growing along the south side of the square.

Even the *carabinieri* might have heard about Father Rico who felt it was his job to help the needy and the downtrodden. The priest, at times, biked along the railway tracks until he would reach a cattle train stopped not too far from the station. When he would look up at the high slits that served as windows under the metal roof, he saw hands grasping at bars. The train would soon leave, heading for death camps with its human cargo of pain and suffering. Aiming past the bars, Father Rico would toss pieces of bread and chunks of cheese at the frantic hands. He could not ignore the innocent, the hungry men and women and the crying children crammed inside the death train.

He risked his own life going near the train station. Were he caught helping Jews, he would be jailed, tortured, then executed by a firing squad. But that didn't stop him.

One evening, he was going through his rosary when someone knocked on his door. Don Rico hastened to open it. A thin girl stood waiting by the door frame.

"May I?" She was panting as if she had run all the way to the cathedral.

"Sure, Maura," the priest replied, swinging the door wide open.

She stepped in and shut the door behind. She pushed her long hair behind her ear. Sunk deep into their sockets, her dark eyes made her face look pale, as if she had been inside the house for too long. "They're looking for me."

"Who is that?" Father Rico asked, but he already knew the answer.

"Renzo and his men."

Maura was the niece of the chief of police, Renzo Felloni, who thought he was a big wheel in the Fascist Party during the atrocities of World War II. Against her uncle's advice, she started dating a neighbour who was a Jew. Everyone warned her about the danger she could face. Soldiers might show up one night at her doorstep and arrest her for collaborating or consorting with *enemies of the state*. She believed her uncle would rescue her from the accusations and she didn't expect he would be the first one to point his finger at her. Renzo picked her up. Back at his place, he grabbed her and tore off her dress. He slapped her around and beat her. He handcuffed her to the bedposts, took a garden hose and gave her an icy cold shower. With brush and soap, he scrubbed and washed and cleaned her as if she were a dirty whore. She would have to be ready for him. For him alone. No one else could touch her creamy white breasts and her smooth thighs. He couldn't resist her beauty. And he would have to make sure she wouldn't see her boyfriend ever again. Renzo wanted to keep her under control and he believed he knew how.

"I could chain you inside the cage perched high on the brick tower," he whispered in her ear.

"Why don't you?"

Renzo was in a top command position and many people depended upon his decisions. He couldn't let his favourite niece get involved with a Jew. Or even worse, allow her to marry a Jew. Renzo often warned her to stop going out with her boyfriend and she should have listened.

Through torture and interrogation, Renzo would make political prisoners confess what they didn't want to let him know. He would round up Jews and Partisans to be sent to the gas chambers of the death camps.

Renzo became rich by pocketing cash and jewels from Jewish homes without asking anyone else's permission. He was without a conscience and he looted whenever he felt like it. At times, he would promise to help those in danger and he would get paid, only to send them to their deaths.

One day, his men picked up Maura's boyfriend, Ezio, as he was about to leave his house to go to school. At the police station, an enraged Renzo punched and kicked Ezio until he blacked out.

Maura didn't have a hope in hell to see her friend ever again. She went to the police station and begged Renzo to let Ezio go free.

"He's not here," Renzo replied.

"Where is he?" she asked him.

"None of your business." Renzo hammered the top of his desk with his chunky fist.

"You've no right to do what you please with him. He's

a decent human being. And you . . . ."

"Didn't do anything."

"Why would you send him to his death?"

"Shut up. Bitch!" He took a wire hanger and assaulted Maura again.

Bleeding, she returned to her apartment. But when an army truck halted near the front door, Maura watched the black-booted soldiers march to the entrance. She climbed up the ladder to the attic, punched the wooden trap door open and squeezed through, heading for the red-tiled roof.

Crawling on her hands and knees on top of the tiled roof, she heard the soldiers kick in the door to search her apartment. Maura stretched out to grasp the neighbour's eavestrough. Her body jammed tight like a sardine, she was sandwiched, hidden between the two stone buildings. She managed to remain undetected behind the blackened chimney when the soldiers searched the roof. Later, she crept along the eavestroughs and slid down the rainwater pipe running down the side of the edifice.

She raced along *Via Giustiziati*, Street of the Executed. She shivered when she approached the earth-brown brick *Torre della Gabbia*, the Tower of the Cage where criminals used to be locked up, in the extreme summer heat or in the freezing winter cold, and left to die when the Gonzagas ruled over Mantova five centuries ago. People believed there was something sinister about that tower and they avoided that street. If they had to walk by the tower, they would cross the street to stay away from the structure which projected its long shadow, a claw of a giant raven chasing after them. Some townsfolk swore that the chief of police would execute political prisoners by tying a couple of them together and placing them upside down inside the cage at night when the bats would peck at their eyes and bite their ears off.

Maura was out of breath, rushing past the tower. She turned around to make sure no one followed her. The soldiers wouldn't be anxious to chase her near the tower. She couldn't stop running until she reached the rectory. Father Rico was the only one who could save her life. She felt bad about what happened to her, but she knew the priest would never condemn her no matter what.

Her feet were bleeding when she arrived at Don Rico's door. The priest fed her some milk and almond biscuits. He prepared a cot down in the wine cellar and he gave her a brown woolen blanket to keep warm.

The church cellar was a safe refuge for a Jew or a *partigiano* who needed to go underground before slipping away and crossing the Alps into a neutral country like Switzerland. A fugitive could sleep on a straw cot stretched out between empty barrels. In the morning, the cot would be rolled up and hidden behind the purple wine barrels which stood along the packed dirt wall.

If anyone, even a priest like Don Rico, were to be caught helping the Allies or the Resistance, he would be tortured and executed without a trial. The police regarded all Jews, *partigiani* and their collaborators as Communists and traitors to be shot or tortured until they would confess crimes they had never committed. Ripped toenails. Crushed fingernails. Broken bones. Nipples burnt by cigarettes. Live electric wires shocking genitals. Seventy-two-hour non-stop interrogation under bright lamps. No food, no drink, no sleep. God knows what Padre Rico would face if he were picked up and arrested by the police. But the risk didn't scare him. Helping people like Maura was worth it.

She had the cellar all to herself at the time and she read books such as *The Betrothed* by Alessandro Manzoni.

She was interested in the two lovers who found themselves stuck in Milan when the black plague hit the city and the surrounding areas. The plague mowed down people like flies. No one was immune. The two lovers were supposed to get married, but faced more obstacles each day. Maura had nightmares about their predicament. She couldn't sleep. In the middle of the night, the air raids would scare her with some heavy bombings aimed at the cathedral. The walls would shake with the loud explosions echoing within the cellar. Pregnant, Maura was worried.

If the place would cave in, she would be buried under a ton of rubble. Her uncle would never dig through the debris to look for her. He couldn't care less if she survived or not. Also, she didn't want to be captured, only to become her uncle Renzo's pawn once again.

Renzo had been Rico's friend. They had attended high school together. Renzo used to copy Rico's Latin homework to have good marks until their teacher got mad and suspended them both for a couple of days. Renzo played hooky for two weeks and dropped out for the rest of the year. Rico returned to school and had to write "*Mea culpa*" a hundred times, but he did not quit.

Renzo Felloni decided to pay an unexpected visit to his old school friend at the rectory on a sunny afternoon. Padre Rico let him in and invited him to sit down in the small *sala* located not too far from the kitchen and the hidden trap door leading to the cellar. The same *sala* served also as an office to meet members of the Christian community. An old breviary kept the priest's desk straight and leveled by filling the gap between a stumpy leg and the hardwood floor. Renzo bumped into the desk and his pockmarked face wrinkled into a frown as he almost fell over the unsteady desk which threatened to topple over his toes.

"What's this? A trap? Jeeeez!" Renzo swore, stomping and searching the room as if he were stuck inside a cage. He couldn't find anything suspicious and sat down.

Father Rico served him some *vino bianco*. "Try this."

"Can't drink wine without any food." Renzo patted his stomach. "Got anything to eat?"

"How would you like a *panino*?" Rico offered him buns and some *pecorino* cheese sliced very thin.

Renzo bit into the crust of a bun. "Too hard to eat," he said, but took another bite and stuffed more cheese into his mouth. "You have enough food here to feed an army." He shook his head and grabbed another bun.

"Many hungry people stop here for a bite to eat."

"Your job is to look after people's souls. Not after their bodies."

"How can you separate the body from the soul?"

"Awwwright. Feed the body and starve the soul, hah?" Renzo gulped down a mouthful of wine. "This wine tastes smoky. Dull. Flat." Renzo spat a mixture of saliva and wine into a crumpled handkerchief. His bushy eyebrows matched the rust-brown colour of his bristly sideburns. "Don't you have anything else for me to drink?"

"That's all I have, Renzo, unless you'd like some fresh water from the busy fountain in *Broletto Square*." The priest pointed to a green bottle. "Here it is. Cool. Delicious. Went to fetch it this morning. It doesn't have that awful taste of rust, like the water from the tap."

"Don't like water. I'd rather have wine. As red as blood. It makes your own blood spring to life and you feel strong. Feeds your body, ready to move mountains." With his right hand, Renzo stroked his left sideburn.

"Have only a bit of white wine."

"Red is vigorous, robust. Husky."

"What difference does that make? Wine is wine." Don Rico poured himself some water.

Renzo wheezed. From a small box, he took out a pinch of tobacco to chew. "Have to change that awful taste your wine left in my mouth."

The priest raised his glass and gulped down half his water. "Hah, this is God's gift. Better than wine any time. Cheaper too."

"If you don't appreciate wine, you have no right to keep the *vino bianco* locked away," Renzo thundered, like he was concerned about the community and all the people who went hungry every day to feed the army in a war that could only maim or kill them. He shoved his chair against the wall. "You don't need that wine."

Father Rico swallowed more water. "Need wine just to celebrate the *Santa Messa*, the Holy Mass," he said. "It's for the Sacrament of the Holy Communion." He was worried. If Renzo would ever search the cellar, Maura would be in trouble. She was too big to fit into an empty wine barrel and hide.

Pacing the room, the chief of police grunted. "Huh!" He folded his yellowed kerchief and wiped the tobacco juice from the sides of his mouth. "How much wine do you have? A barrel? Or two?"

"Half barrel."

"You don't have to make your whole congregation drink. Do you? Dammit! We're going to have a bunch of drunks."

"Couldn't give a drink to everyone. Most parishioners get fresh water at the fountain." The priest reddened like a novice preaching his first sermon.

"Just worry about their souls, will you?"

"Can't quench everybody's thirst. Not with white wine

anyway." Don Rico glanced at the wine bottle. It was almost empty. "But with God's help, I'll do what I can to look after their souls." He was afraid that Renzo would want more wine and push his way down to the cellar.

"It's your own flock. Do what you want with it." Renzo sneezed. "Have to send down two of my men to pick up the wine. They're always busy. But this is important. First on my list," he grumbled, poured the rest of the wine and drained his glass. He slapped Rico's shoulder with his fleshy hand and marched out of the room. He slammed the door shut and the walls shook in the rectory.

Don Rico breathed with relief. He might be forced to hand his wine over to Renzo and his men, but he wouldn't want to betray Maura. Her uncle would be harsher with her than with anybody else. There was only bad blood between them. Nothing could ever change that. Renzo and his men would put her in jail. Torture her. Don Rico thought she should leave right away before the police would return to pick up the wine.

The priest prepared a basket with some bread and *pecorino* for her lunch. He would lend her his bike to ride out of town and it would be best if she wore an old pair of pants. By now, she was bulky enough to pass as a man.

Maura found out she would have to travel out of town and wait until night. She didn't like to face such a long journey in the dark. She would have to watch out for land mines or vipers. Also, she didn't want to be stopped by the soldiers patrolling the area, or they would arrest her. She didn't mind, however, the idea of living in the country with Father Rico's aunt, Nerina, who would be waiting for her at her farm. Maura could cook and do some sewing to pay for her room and board.

From a secret pocket sewn on the inside of her shirt,

Maura pulled out a chain with the star Ezio had given her before he was picked by the secret police.

"See this, Padre? It's the gift my boyfriend gave me before he was taken away," she said as she was about to leave. "I want you to have it for all you have done for me."

"Ezio escaped. He's in the country. His precious gift means more to you than anything else in the world," he replied. "Keep it. You might need it one day."

Maura took the basket with bread and *pecorino*. She slipped out the door and started pedaling to go out of town. She would look for Ezio. Riding alone on a lonely stretch of road, she was scared that night. No light was allowed during the curfew. Like a thin slice of honeydew melon, a crescent moon shed an amber gleam upon the countryside. The stars glittered, pins piercing through the dark pillow of the night sky. Fearful of falling into an ambush, Maura watched the ditch on one side of the road and the tall thick hedge on the other. Soldiers could jump out suddenly from the nearby grove of oak trees and capture her.

Before dawn, she felt the first contractions. She understood she was in labour. She forced herself to keep on heading to the farm, where she would find a big-boned woman with brown eyes and a throaty laugh.

Maura hoped to arrive at Nerina's farm soon, but she couldn't ride her bike any longer. She pushed her bicycle over the shoulder of the highway and went past the thorny hedge. She didn't want to give birth in the middle of the road and she began cutting through a nearby field.

She crossed the muddy field and stumbled over a few lumps of dirt. Her left foot got caught in a wiry snag that triggered the explosion of a land mine. The blast shook the ground. Like a meteorite, it tore open a deep hole. The detonation sent Maura flying into a bushy thicket full of thorns. Bleeding from a cut on her ankle and a gash near her left temple, she attempted to bandage her wounds with her scarf. She was in shock. She bit her tongue. The pains of labour made her weep. Sparks had ignited the dry grass. She was afraid that the soldiers patrolling the road might have heard the explosion and they would soon arrive. They might arrest her and take away her baby.

Maura didn't want to give up. When she heard some steps, she pulled down the branches of a shrub to conceal herself behind a patch of prickly thistles.

The moon in the sky shone brighter and the flames were crackling closer to her. Maura was afraid to be dis-covered. A cramp tightened her abdomen and she took a deep breath to stop herself from screaming.

A big woman rushed to the fire licking the ground. It was Nerina who had been awakened by the explosion near her farm. When she saw the flames devouring the turf by the hedge, she rushed to the ditch to draw water with her pail and put out the fire.

The thick smoke from the burnt grass stung her nostrils as Nerina managed to toss enough water to smother the flames. A moan made her rush to Maura lying within the thorny thicket. She had never expected to find her in labour. Maura was still alive, but her pulse felt weak.

"Father Rico," she murmured.

Aunt Nerina understood she needed help. "Push. One more push," she said.

"Haaaaaawww!" Maura yelled as the head of the baby showed up first and then the tiny body slipped out with a whoosh.

Nerina grabbed the baby. "It's a boy," she whispered. Dawn streaked the sky with a pinkish glow.

Maura cried. "It's like a ray of sun," she gasped as she

held her baby to her breast. "Ray of sun. Raimondo."

"Ray. Raymond," Nerina said. "Great name."

Maura pulled out the gold chain and star from her pouch and let it dangle closer to her baby. "One day, this treasure is going to be yours." She felt ready to face anything as she cradled the baby in her arms. She glanced at the violet clouds roaming across the sky. With a sigh, she handed her baby over to Nerina.

Nerina couldn't move Maura by herself. She would have to find some help. First, she carried home the baby who was crying. The newborn was hungry and Nerina would give him some milk. She lived alone ever since she had lost her husband when a workhorse, scared by an army tank rolling down the road, kicked him in the head and split his cranium in two. Nerina had always wanted to have a child, but she would never have the chance to raise any offspring of her own. She cuddled the baby in her arms until he fell sound asleep. She felt guilty about abandoning the wounded mother in the field that night. Nerina didn't know if she was still bleeding, but she vowed to look after Maura until she would get well. With her farmhand, she returned bringing a homemade stretcher she had built with a blanket fastened to two long sticks. They carried Maura to the farm house where it was warm and cozy.

Maura had grown up like a reckless tomboy. She liked to climb trees, chasing after squirrels or chipmunks and she spent her summer in a tree house her uncle built for her on his farm. Uncle Renzo would help her climb up, but he would often take the ladder away and she had to wait until he brought it back. Once, she tried to go down on her own, but a small branch gave way under her weight and she fell, scraping her elbows and knees raw. A broken branch cut her near the eye. It was a miracle she didn't lose her sight.

Sometimes, Renzo would beat her and punish her for disobeying him. She was too afraid of him and wouldn't tell anyone about those incidents. She loved the outdoors, but she didn't want to return to his farm.

When she turned into an attractive girl, with her green eyes and the peach and cream complexion of a teen in bloom, Maura tried to avoid Renzo. She wanted to go out with her boyfriend, Ezio. If she ran away from home, her uncle would get his men to search the fields to find her. Renzo swore she would forget her boyfriend soon, or he would be jailed and sent to a concentration camp.

She believed her boyfriend's presence would discourage Renzo from going after her. But often Renzo stood for a long time at the corner near her school and waited for her. He would force her to go out of town against her will. She couldn't even tell her mother about this. People talked and her mother was a strict Catholic who didn't like the idea of her daughter going steady with her boyfriend. Ezio belonged to a stern Jewish family and Maura's mother believed her brother Renzo was right to keep an eye on her daughter. When Maura began dating Ezio, her mother wanted to lock her inside the house or send her to a convent.

Maura disappeared and Renzo searched everywhere for her. But no one had seen her. He heard the rumour she had been involved in some kind of trouble. Nobody told him about the baby. Had Renzo known about the newborn, he would take his revenge.

Maura didn't mind staying with her baby at Nerina's farm where there was food for both of them. She could even breast-feed her baby without worrying about soldiers breaking in. She regained her strength within a few weeks and knew she might face Renzo one day, but she was not afraid.

When she got well, she went to visit Don Rico still recovering at the hospital after his awful accident near the square. A pungent smell of ether and disinfectant lingered in the hallway, where a strange hush couldn't hide the hurt and suffering inside the dim-lit rooms. In their leaf-green uniforms, three or four nurses rushed along the corridor.

A brunette was bent over the wooden counter and her white-trimmed crest shivered on top of her head as she nodded to Maura. The brunette gestured to a tall nurse who shuffled around on sturdy legs, leading Maura further down the long white-walled corridor.

The tall nurse's feet floated inside her white shoes, the size of two skis. Maura had to hurry to catch up to her as they approached Father Rico's room.

His face whiter than the sheets, Rico grinned and sat up when he saw Maura standing hesitantly at the foot of his bed.

"Hi!"

"Maura." The priest waved her closer to him. "How did you find me?"

"Easy. Everyone in town talks about you."

"Do they wonder why the truck didn't stop?"

"Guess so. It's scary for everyone."

"I think that crazy driver was drunk." Rico punched his white pillow and propped himself up onto his right elbow. "Ready to pass out."

"Why would you have to suffer if he was drunk?" Maura sighed. "It's that insane driver who has to pay. Not you."

"Don't say that. I forgive him." Don Rico tugged at a corner of his blanket. He had lost his suntan and he appeared weak and frail. "My foot was in very bad shape." He motioned with his hand to his left leg, still under the blanket. But Maura didn't want to look, as if she were afraid of what she might find.

She bowed her head. "I've heard."

"The word spreads around faster than the funnel of a whirlwind, if something bad happens in this town." Father Rico slapped his mattress. "Doctors amputated my foot. But no one can touch my soul. They can't cut out a piece. It's whole. And better than ever."

"Right!" As she bent over and pulled up a chair, the gold chain and star dangled from her neck.

Father Rico noticed it. "You still have your gold chain. Good thing you wear it."

She fingered her chain. "It kept me and my baby safe."

"Think so?" Father Rico's eyes lit up.

Maura touched his hand. "Thank you for what you've done for me and Ezio. You risked your life."

"But you deserve all the help I could give you."

"How's that?"

"You've bridged the gap between two different cultures. You know that one could not rule out the other. You try to make people understand both, coming to terms with one another." His firm voice echoed within the bare walls of the room as if he were giving an important sermon to his congregation during Mass in church.

"Maybe I've learned from you to care about people regardless of gender, race or creed." Maura pursed her lips, tugging at her gold chain. "Wish I could do much more."

Don Rico's eyes gleamed like smoldering coals about to flare up once more. "So do I."

Maura clenched her fists. "Sometimes I feel sad if I can not help someone in need." Her nails dug into her palms.

Don Rico folded the white blanket over his legs like a

wide bandage. "God can see beyond all our problems," he said. "He gives us the strength to live through the toughest tests. See?" He unrolled the blanket and tore it off. His left leg was a bandaged stump.

Maura puckered her lips. She sat still on the hard chair beside Don Rico's bed. She could not talk or move. Heavy steps could be heard in the hallway. A shadow darkened the entrance and a bulky shape stood at the doorway. It was Renzo.

"Whaaat?" He glared at Maura, then he glanced at Don Rico's bandaged stump.

The priest punched his pillow, doubled it and slid it under his head.

"No choice, Renzo."

Maura shook her finger at her uncle. "You should feel bad. You." She sprang up and jumped between them as if she meant to protect the priest from Renzo. The gold chain sparkled around her neck. "You're responsible for this! I know it was you. Look at what you did."

"He didn't mean it." Rico shook his head. He turned and stared at Renzo. "You couldn't do this to your old friend, could you?"

"No, Rico! You know I'm always busy with my men." He waved his fist. "You don't understand. Christ! I've no-thing to do with this." He bent over the gauze-wrapped stump and he shut his eyes.

"I forgive you." Rico murmured, blessing him with the sign of the cross. "*In Nomine Patri . . . .*"

Renzo twitched his eyebrows and gestured at Maura. "What about her? The cause of all the trouble!" He twisted to the side, grasped her gold chain and tugged hard. But the chain didn't break.

"Let go!" Maura pried his fingers open. "It's mine."

"Don't think so. You must give it to the state for the war effort. Wear an iron chain. Like everyone else." Renzo grabbed Maura's arm and shoved it behind her back.

She cried out in pain. "Ouch!"

"Heh! Who gave you this chain? A dumb boyfriend?"

"Leave her alone." Don Rico tossed his blanket over Renzo's head.

The tall nurse rushed in, paddling around in her ski-like shoes. "What's going on here?"

Groping from inside the blanket, Renzo raised his arms above his head. He tugged until he wrenched himself free and threw the blanket onto the floor. He darted out of the room.

"Wait, hey!" the nurse yelled.

Maura chased after him, running along the corridor. Renzo squeezed between two food carts. His jacket caught on the corner of the cart carrying tea and juices.

"Oooops!" Cups filled with orange juice went flying, drenching Renzo's pants and spilling the rest of their contents on the bluish-veined tiles of the floor.

"Stop!" Maura screamed as a couple of patients peered out of their rooms. "Stop that man."

Renzo hopped over a large puddle of orange juice, but tripped on the hairy head of a mop abandoned against the wall. "Huh?"

He stepped over the mop pail and raced down the hall. He jabbed at the exit door and hurried downstairs.

Maura followed him and rushed down the stairs to the landing on the main floor. But Renzo flew out of the side door leading to the parking lot.

A green car was backing up. The driver was Maura's boyfriend. He braked hard, but couldn't stop the car on time. The bumper pinned Renzo against a parked vehicle.

"Jesus!" Renzo shouted, his pockmarked face turning purple. "What are you doing? Move your dumb car!"

Ezio looked out the driver's window. "Couldn't stop." He stared at a square-jawed Renzo whose head lolled on his double chin as if he were a rag puppet.

"Can't move," he whined.

Maura shot out of the side door. She hurried to the moaning Renzo. "Go ahead!" She waved to her boyfriend whose fingers squeezed the steering wheel as if he were about to drive off.

"The pain." Renzo's face was darkening to a blue tinge. His hooded eyelids drooped.

"You shouldn't have run over Don Rico's foot. People saw you driving the hit-and-run army truck that morning." Maura glared at the groaning Renzo. "And Ezio! You were going to send him to his death."

"Didn't mean to." Renzo whimpered as Ezio drove his car ahead. Renzo's body went limp like a huge lump of jelly. Maura hugged him to keep him standing. She helped the tall nurse carry him back inside the hospital.

A stern-looking intern examined Renzo's wound. The diagnosis was bad. An immediate operation was needed to repair the damage to his legs. Renzo's features darkened. The stubble on his chin looked grey in patches. He scowled and touched his legs to make sure they were still there.

"It hurts bad." He grimaced.

Rico was learning to walk with an artificial limb that he would later hide under his black cassock. He didn't mind visiting Renzo still recuperating from his operation. Rico walked with a slight limp, but Renzo didn't even notice it when the priest entered his hospital room.

"Do you think I'd need Extreme Unction, or something?" Renzo greeted him with a frown.

"Just dropped in to visit," Rico replied.

"Don't bother." His acne scarred face grimaced showing a net of purple veins pulsating as if he had just finished a marathon race.

"Sounds like you're your old self again."

"What do you mean?"

"You're doing well enough to get mad at me." Don Rico stepped beside Renzo's bed.

"Can look after myself," Renzo grunted.

"God wants you to."

"God? Who? He ties us down. Sends us to hell."

"The Lord lets us free so we can earn our own place in Paradise. Or we'd have no merit. We must work hard to go to Heaven." Rico stared at Renzo who rested against two pillows, his hands tugging at the top sheet like it was a rope he wanted to tear apart.

"It figures." He wrung his sheet.

Rico bowed closer to Renzo's ear. "Haven't seen you at church for months."

"Didn't have time."

"But you had enough time to run over my foot."

"Didn't mean any harm."

"Think I saw *you* driving that army truck."

"You're still here. Alive."

"Why didn't you stop?"

"The truck went out of control." Renzo was wringing his sheets. "My men were waiting at the station."

"God let me live long enough to forgive you." Rico stared at Renzo and poked his bushy chest with one finger. "Wish I could see you in church sometime."

"I'd go right now, if had back my legs. Or even one of them."

Rico bowed his head. "I can bring you Holy Communion, if you confess right here."

"Confess? What?"

"Wouldn't hurt a girl like your niece, would you?"

"Never did." Renzo rubbed the greying stubble on his chin. He had lost weight and his face had acquired a sallow unhealthy colour. But he put his nose high up in the air. He still behaved as if he could control people's lives.

"You hurt her bad."

"Didn't." Renzo tapped his fingers together and made a sort of a basket with them.

"Tell me the truth."

"What do you want to hear?"

"She told me everything." Rico nodded as Renzo looked away. "Don't you worry. I won't tell anyone. Not even her boyfriend."

"You got it all wrong." Renzo's cheeks turned purple. "Dammit! What about her damned boyfriend who pinned my legs in between two vehicles?"

"He must find the strength to take care of Maura and her baby."

"Her baby, hah? That bastard."

"What kind of a Catholic are you? How can you talk like that?"

"Who cares?"

"The Lord."

"I'm not worried about God."

"He's worried about you." Rico sighed. "You can't even take care of *your* child. You should at least ask Maura to forgive you."

"Maura had it coming to her. She's stupid like all those other women." Renzo punched his pillow. Although he looked thinner, he still had his quivering double chin.

"The women might understand and find out the truth," Don Rico stretched out his arms.

"Must throw them in jail. Lock them inside that cage high up on the tower and toss the keys into the lake."

"God won't let you." Rico took Renzo's hand and he didn't struggle. "Maura told me she forgives you."

"Let's forget about her." Renzo bowed his head.

Renzo's knee stumps gangrened and he had several other operations after the war. No wonder he never gets out of his wheelchair and he does not wish to see anyone.

Maura doesn't visit him. She finished college and she took over my grandmother's duties at church. She often assists Father Rico in organizing special celebrations.

Ezio owns his own bakery and he hires many delivery boys. He makes sure Father Rico's congregation always has fresh bread and pastry to eat every day.

If Ezio understands what went on, a long time ago, in the hidden office of the chief of secret police, he doesn't let anyone know. And that won't stop him from living his own life the best he can with his wife and children, Raymond and baby Nerina.

Thistle Creek

PART TWO:

I Can't Complain

It was a cold day in March. Snow fell mixed with rain, coating the road with ice. I was new in the city and I didn't know how nasty the weather could get. A bad chill could get me into trouble and I couldn't afford to get sick. I pulled up the hood of my old suede coat over my head. It would be ruined in the half-frozen sleet, but I didn't care. I wore that coat for far too many winters and it was coming apart under the armpits. I had to tug at the edge of the hood to cover my head or my hair would become all wet and curl up like a roll of rusty chicken wire. Usually, I pull up my hair with barrettes, shaping it into a chignon at night, and I must work hard to keep it straight.

I zippered up Darrin's blue-trimmed parka and placed him beside me on the front seat of my car. We faced a long drive and I gave him a cookie to keep him occupied. His chubby little cheeks swelled up as he nibbled at his chocolate chip cookie and watched the sleet slide down the windshield. He stuck his thumb in his mouth when he finished the cookie.

With my right hand, I pulled at the top of a plastic bag stuffed into my purse.

"Here . . . Take another cookie," I said. Stretching out my arm, I tugged at his thumb. "And get that out of your mouth."

He started to cry. "Nooo, noooo," he wailed.

I patted him on the head. I wanted to keep him quiet as I drove away from the small suburban home I rent by the month. We were heading for the Duggan Health Clinic where Darrin was supposed to get his booster shots for measles and whooping cough. I couldn't take him to the clinic the next day. I had to start working at *Between Green Onions*, a nearby restaurant where I would serve subs, pizza pies, spaghetti and spinach-green *tortellini*.

The engine missed a beat and sounded as if it had hiccups. Suddenly, my car jerked up like a bucking horse. It went off the road. I slammed on the brakes, but couldn't stop my Toyota. It skidded over the thin coat of black ice and slid into the ditch. I thought we were sinking into quicksand and I was scared. How would we ever get out? When the front tires hit a chunky stone, the car shook and came to a halt with a big jolt. Stuck. I was trembling, but I turned the key in the ignition and tried to start the stalled engine. I pushed the gas pedal right down to the floor and made another attempt to get the motor started. The engine sent out only a gurgle. Nothing worked. Tied with his seat belt, Darrin squirmed, kicked and screamed. His little face became as red as a ripe pepper.

"Shhh!" I put my index finger on my lips. "Shhhh!"

"Mmmaaa!" he yelled out, tears rolling down his round cheeks. "Mmmaaaa!"

I got out, unfastened Darrin's seat belt, took him in my arms and locked my stalled Toyota. I began walking on the shoulder of the road, staying as close as possible to the muddy ditch. With every step, my boots seemed to become heavier, as if made of wet clay.

An approaching motorist, driving a station wagon, swerved and kept on going. The road was very slippery and

I didn't want to flag him down. I'd risk getting run over by a car out of control.

I stepped into the freezing slush stretching along the bottom of the ditch. Another driver was slowing down as if to stop his Escort, but didn't. His engine picked up with a roar and his tires spun on the crust of ice. Everybody had a hard time just trying to keep their vehicles on the road.

Heading north toward the busy Whitemud Freeway, I trudged along the shoulder of 111 Street. Darrin slowly calmed down, but he was squeezing my neck too tight. It would be a long walk to reach the closest homes. I ploughed through the slush, put Darrin down and rested for a few minutes, then picked him up again to continue my trek.

I climbed up three steps to knock on the door of a brand new bungalow. There was no answer. Nobody home, I guessed as I went on. At the next two-storey home, I rang the bell. A dog started to growl and bark from inside the house. Darrin tugged tight at my hood with both hands, then hugged my neck. I had a rough time breathing.

A gruff man stuck his head out. "Yeah?" A crop of black hair grew on top of his head and matched his dark eyebrows that grew bristly like thorny shrubs. The pit bull snarled, baring its stained teeth. "Get down, Rhino," he warned, turning to the dog. "Down." Jumping up, the animal stuck its front paws onto the man's thighs and nuzzled his groin. "Down, boy. Yeah!"

"My car!" I motioned down the road.

"Stalled?"

"No. Just . . . ."

"Stuck, huh?"

I nodded. "Think so."

"Sorry. But there is nothing I can do for you right now," the man rasped, clutching the pit bull's short-haired brown neck and stroking its steel-studded collar. "My wife went shopping for groceries and I'm baby-sitting with Rhino. Can't leave the house."

The pit bull was growling louder than before, trying to wriggle out of the man's grasp. Froth formed around its huge red mouth as the animal showed off its mandibles and snapped at us. Darrin started to pout and sob. I turned to leave and the door slammed shut.

I stumbled going down the steps of the front porch, but I managed to grab the wooden railing with my right hand. Darrin tightened his grip and almost choked me. He began pulling my hair. I pushed a few strands under my hood as I kept on walking to the next house.

It was a stucco house with a green trim around the pitched roof. I opened the screen door to knock. A slim woman in wranglers answered us. Her hair, the colour of ripe wheat, shook lightly near her face like the frills of her caramel blouse and her eyes shone as if they were two round spots of fresh blue paint on a creamy-white canvas.

"Come in," she said. "Come on in."

I stepped onto a wine-red carpet covering the beige linoleum. "Thanks! Nice and warm in here." I smiled. The fragrance of baked muffins wafted from the kitchen and I swallowed some saliva.

"How can I help you?"

"My car went in the ditch."

"That's too bad." She sighed and stared at us. "Would you like to use the phone?" She waved her right hand. "It's down the hall."

I took off my boots. "Thanks. Have to call a tow truck. I'm new in the city and I don't know too many people."

"Why don't you let me try to get your car out of the ditch?" She tilted her head to one side and smiled. "I have booster cables. And chains with a hook to pull your car out. Bet we could even drive it out."

"Sounds good," I said, but I still was not sure whether we could drag my Toyota out of the ditch without a tow truck. "It's nasty outside, but we can try."

A toffee Siamese raced into the hall and stopped to look us over with its slanted indigo eyes. Darrin giggled and stretched out his right arm to reach for the cat's furry tail.

"Let's get something for you." The woman winked at Darrin who was busy twisting to one side to touch the cat's tail. "You're a good boy."

She led us into the kitchen and served us muffins that were still hot from the oven. They tasted like wheat and honey. Darrin drank some chocolate milk which pasted a moustache on his upper lip.

"Tasty muffins," I said.

"I baked some for my daughter, Khristyn. She likes to nibble at some new goodies each time she comes home from school."

"Are you sure you have enough time to pull my Toyota out of the ditch before Khristyn returns home?"

"Khristyn has the key." The woman took her black wool coat and nodded to the door leading to the garage. "We'll fetch my tools." She waved to me. "There is a shovel you may need to free your tires from the grip of the snow."

On the way out, I grabbed my boots. "If you have a bag of sand it might help me to get some traction on the ice."

The woman bent over and picked up a bag of sand in the corner of the garage. "Here we are. We'll pull your car out in no time. Let's go. We've got work to do."

As I put Darrin on the back seat of her green Mustang, he was still chewing his muffin. But he stopped when he noticed the growling pit bull zigzagging down the street.

The short-tailed animal wobbled on the road, heading for the Mustang. The large mouth was covered with froth as if the dog had rabies. With a leap, the dog lurched at the Siamese cat dashing to hide behind my feet. I stooped, swept up the Siamese and slipped it back into the house. I rushed back to the vehicle as the woman revved the engine, frightening the angry dog. I got in the car and I slammed the passenger door shut.

"Just in time." She nodded.

"Your neighbour should lock up his pit bull," I said. "Or else we'll have to put it in jail at the dog pound."

She laughed. "Shimsyn isn't afraid of that pit bull and follows me every time I go out. That stubborn cat wants to fight. Unless it's waiting for Khristyn to come home from school. There, she is now."

A little girl in a pink and green parka was hopping over the slushy puddles. The pit bull was sniffing around the nearest lamppost, but turned around. The car was moving as I jumped out and rushed through the sludge.

I reached for the school girl in green rubber boots. Her face was flushed. "Hi, Khristyn." I grabbed her and brought her with me inside the Mustang creeping along the curb.

"Hi, sweetie!" The woman sighed.

"Mum, I'm hungry," Khristyn said. She stared at Darrin still munching on the back seat.

He took his half-chewed muffin and handed it over to Khristyn who giggled as if she had found her best friend. The sleet was pelting the windshield. It was turning the wet snow into slush. The wind whistled, blowing hard drizzle against the shell of the Mustang. I wondered how this car would ride on the slippery road. The motor sounded groggy, but kept purring.

On the back seat, Darrin fell asleep with his thumb in

his mouth. He sucked in his chubby little cheeks and I didn't want to wake him up.

"You're all wet."

"I'm already drying up," the girl said as a few chestnut curls shook on her temple. "Look."

"Too bad the weather's so nasty," I said.

The woman pulled Khristyn closer to her. "Don't you worry. The storm will soon be over."

Both mother and daughter were right. Now, the worst of the storm is gone and to tell the truth I can't complain.

Awakening

My mother was still asleep when I awoke at sunrise that day. It was early spring and my mother always got up before anyone else in our family, but that morning she lay motionless on her bed like an eggshell porcelain statue. Resting on her back, she slept without making a sound. I couldn't hear her breathe and I was scared.

The grey light of dawn sliced through the curtains to reach my mother's bed. She looked feverish. Her cheeks were wax-white, her eyelids shut. My bed stood not far from hers and I unrolled my blankets to slide out without making any noise. Barefoot on the floor, I felt shivers pricking down my spine. I grabbed my ocher skirt and blouse from the straight-back chair at the foot of my bed.

The floorboards creaked and the furnace went on with a whir. I turned to see if my mother was still asleep. She didn't move, but her breathing sounded like a muffled whistle. Strange. She had never made that kind of noise before. My mother wouldn't usually snore. She would get up at dawn, prepare some hot chocolate and send me off to school. But this morning she seemed sound asleep. It was getting late and I put on my clothes. I tugged at the sheets and pulled the blankets over my pillow to make my bed. My mother always had a light sleep and when rustling of clothes or shuffling of feet could be heard in the bedroom, she would wake up. But this time she continued to sleep.

I listened to her breathing climb to a high-pitched tone vibrating like a shaky note coming from a flute. The sound turned into a gasping noise, as if something was stuck deep down in her throat and she couldn't breathe. My teeth began chattering. Furrows dug deep into her forehead and she looked worn-out. Tired. Exhausted. I wanted to wake her up but I didn't dare.

What happened? Did she stay up, awake, most of the night waiting for my father to get home?

My mother's mouth opened and she wheezed. Her lips quivered. I froze. She had trouble breathing. I was afraid she would choke. Taking a step closer to her bed, I bent over her. I glanced at the blue veins throbbing on her neck and I took her hand in mine. Her palm felt warm and sweaty. I squeezed her hand, but she didn't stir. A cramp crushed my empty stomach.

On the night table, a pitcher half-full of water stood beside a pear-shaped snifter and a small brown bottle lay on its side. Valerian. It was the root extract she had brought from the old country. Tiny, rusty-brown stains dotted the yellowed label. I picked up the little container of Valerian and unscrewed the metal top. Turning the container upside down, I shook it.

Nothing fell out. Not a single caplet. No trace of the twenty-five caplets mentioned on the label. I wanted to scream, but couldn't. My tongue seemed glued to my palate. Another cramp crammed my stomach. I didn't know how to wake my mother. She wheezed and gasped. My hands were trembling. I bent to kiss her forehead and tears blurred my eyes. Her cheeks were sallow and I was worried.

Why didn't she wake up? My fear grew and I couldn't even swallow. "Mamma," I whispered, stroking her warm hand. "Mamma."

I stared at the ivory lace of her nightgown shivering near her throat. My stomach ached and I bit my lip. I didn't want to disturb my mother, but I straightened her blue blanket and pulled it closer to her chin as I tucked her in. She looked weary. Her matted brown hair stuck to the sides of her head and her eyelids seemed stitched together.

She needed help and I had to call my father. Taking a deep breath, I tiptoed out of the bedroom and ran to find him in the other room.

My father would often sleep on the couch in the living room when he came home late at night. Sprawled on top of the cushions, he snored loudly. "Papa . . . Papa," I whispered. I was afraid he would wake up grumpy and shout at me. But he did not hear me. I coughed and couldn't get rid of the bitter taste in my mouth.

"Mamma . . . Mamma doesn't wake up," I cried out and shook his shoulder.

My father rubbed his eyes. "What is it?" He stretched out his arm and pushed me aside. "Let me sleep."

"Mamma's asleep . . . ." I burst into tears.

"Don't cry." He sat up and glanced at his wristwatch. "Time for you to go to school, my dear girl. You'll see your mother later."

"I . . . I can't wake her up," I sobbed.

"Gesú Mio! What's all the fuss?" My father tossed off his striped sable blanket and stood up. His blue shirt looked crumpled and his grey pants creased and frazzled. Sighing, he raked his black hair with his fingers and blinked. The lines near his eyes deepened when he yawned. He scratched his chin and tucked in his shirt.

"Mamma sleeps and won't wake up. She . . . ." I stammered. "She's sick."

My father clenched his fists and shuffled out of the living room, his blue shirt still unbuttoned. I followed him into the bedroom where my mother slept.

"Lucia," he murmured, touching her hand. "Lucia." He clutched the brown bottle of Valerian, turned it upside down and stared at it. "Empty?" His face paled. "These look like the sleeping pills she bought more than a year ago at that little old pharmacy back in her village. How did she manage to bring this stuff along?" Tilting his head to the side, he put the brown container back on the night table and placed his palm over her forehead. "Hhmmphh!" he sighed. "Don't know."

"Papa?" I cried and tugged at his sleeve.

He handed me the little bottle. "Here. Let's keep this to show to the doctor. Put it on top of the dresser."

"No! Papa . . . Why?" I wiped my eyes, clutching the brown bottle in my fist. My heart hammered fast as I placed the empty container on top of the dresser. The bottle stood out like a stick poking out of a big flowerpot.

My father leaned over and untied the bow at my mother's neck. "This knot's too tight." His voice quavered and his hands trembled. "She's got to breathe."

"Papa, what's wrong?"

"We have no time to lose." His fingers fumbled to loosen the ribbon of her nightgown.

"Papa?"

"Have to call an ambulance."

My father rushed back to the living room. He picked up the phone and dialed a few numbers. "Hello! Quick . . . An ambulance . . . quick!" He shouted our address. "That's in Castledown. Not too far from the Yellowhead Trail." He slammed down the receiver and pushed a stool against the wall. When he returned into the bedroom, he stared at my mother's waxen face and tightened his lips. He clasped both hands behind his back and began pacing around the room.

"Papa?"

"We have to wait a few minutes . . . They'll send an ambulance," he said. I tugged at his shirt sleeve and he stopped beside me. He patted my arm. "I'll make some breakfast for you."

"No. Mamma's sick and I want to stay here with her."

"I'll prepare a cup of hot chocolate for you," he murmured and walked out of the bedroom.

My mother wheezed and I glanced at her. I was afraid.

I straightened out her sheets and blankets again and wiped her forehead with a facecloth. My father brought me a big cup full of hot chocolate. "Here. Careful! It's hot." He scratched his neck. "I couldn't find the sugar bowl set." He frowned and stared at me. "Where did it go? Did you see it somewhere around the house?"

"Si . . . Papa. I saw it on the table."

"Hah, I knew we didn't sell it." My father shook his head. "But it's not on the table now."

"No . . . Papa."

"Where did that sugar bowl go?"

"I . . . I'm not sure."

"I brought our radio to a friend to pay some of the bills, but we'll have it back soon." He stared at me. "Now, I can't find that oval silver tray with the creamer and the sugar bowl. Where did they end up? At the pawnshop? You must know."

I shrugged. "Don't think so."

He waved one hand and pointed in the direction of the living room. "I saw the sugar bowl right over there inside the china cabinet, just yesterday . . . ."

I felt a sharp pain kneading my stomach. Crossing my

arms, I thought of the silver tray. I remembered my mother serving coffee to the landlord the day before when I came home from school. It was earlier than usual and I went straight into the kitchen where the smell of espresso coffee hung in the air. The silver set with the creamer and the sugar bowl lay in the middle of the table. My mother sat at one end of the table, her eyes red and puffy. She bowed her head when she saw me.

Signor Pino Baldi, the landlord, grunted and drained his cup of coffee. His short-haired bulldog growled in a corner and bared its yellow teeth at me. A leather-coloured spot stretched from its throat down to its belly. The dog stood up and snapped at us with its huge ugly mouth. The bulldog's tongue loomed scarlet like a beet stuck between two rows of sharp teeth.

"Down, Butch!" Pino grumbled, slapping his own leg. "Get down, away. Sit!" He got up, buttoned his jacket and rubbed the bulldog's neck. Then, he glanced at me and pretended not to see me. The bulldog growled and the landlord bent to tug at the bronze-spiked collar. "Sit!"

I fished out an almond-sprinkled biscuit and a round *amaretto* from the cookie jar and I ran out to play by the front steps. The *amaretto* tasted like honey and walnuts, but it was hard to chew. I dropped my cookie when I heard Signor Pino shout at my mother.

"Cristo! I need the rent now, Lucia." His throaty voice sounded threatening and the dog barked. "I've got taxes and bills to pay. Can't you give me at least part of the rent?"

"We'll pay next week," my mother said. "Lorenzo might get a job and we'll soon have the money."

"Lorenzo, hah! That husband of yours can do nothing better than play poker every night. He's a no good loafer," the landlord yelled, banging on the table as his dog growled.

"He's a hard working man. A good bricklayer. He'll find a job and we'll pay."

"*Dannato cane!* How can I believe you, Lucia? You've been telling me the same story for the past three months, but I haven't seen a cent."

"Things will change and we'll have the rent for you soon," my mother cried out. "We'll catch up. Don't worry."

"Why worry?" A few more bangs and booms could be heard. "I'll take this silver tray . . . ."

"No, no. You can't do that to me! My tray is worth more to me than the rent we owe you."

"I want my money, Lucia. You don't need a silver tray, anyway. I may as well take it with me," the landlord roared. The dog barked louder. "Down Butch! Sit."

"Wait! You can't take that tray without my husband's permission."

"Are you kidding, Lucia? Who needs his permission? Lorenzo wants to move out of here," Signor Pino thundered. "With you, or without you. The manager of a high-rise phoned me the other day. He told me Lorenzo made an application to move into one of his suites on 112 Street and Jasper. The manager asked me if your husband pays his bills and his rent on time. Did you know that?"

"What did you say?"

"I told him he has trouble paying."

"Lorenzo's brother, Remo, asked us to move closer to him. Remo needs some help with his grocery store not far from Jasper Avenue, because he lost his right arm in a bad car accident and his wife is pregnant," my mother said. "They both work hard to keep the store open, but they can't do everything themselves."

"So . . . you people may move out without paying the rent, huh!" Signor Pino shouted and his dog howled. "It doesn't matter how far you move. I'll go after you."

"I wouldn't tell you all this if we planned to move out without paying the rent." My mother coughed. "Lorenzo doesn't want to leave this house, but it's too expensive for us. You gave us a rent increase last month and this place is too far away from his brother's business. A small apartment closer to Remo's grocery store might be cheaper than this place."

"No way. Not there. A suite in a high-rise might cost a lot more than here," the landlord rasped. "And you get no privacy. No tomato patch. Nothing. Not like in this house."

My mother cleared her throat. "My husband wants to help his brother and he will still look for work."

"Your Lorenzo better make up his mind and pay the rent on time, or I'll take the proper steps to evict you."

"We just want to settle down and we need a bit more time. My husband might find work in construction and I'll help his brother run the store. We'll earn the money to pay what we owe you," my mother said. Spoons tinkled like bells hitting cups and saucers. Cupboard doors slammed shut.

"Cristo! No more excuses, Lucia. Give me a clean glass. I need a shot of the *grappa* I brought along. Where's your snifter? Aahhh! There. Try some. It's good for you."

"No. Don't . . . My tray." My mother shrieked and the dog howled. The scraping noises of their struggle followed the dull thud of someone falling to the floor. "Give me back my silver tray."

"I'll take the tray for now." The bulldog barked and whined louder than a bitch in heat. "I'll be back in two days to get the rest of the rent. At least three hundred dollars, Lucia, or you'll have to move out right away." The landlord's voice sounded hoarse and gruff as he threatened my mother, echoing his dog's growl.

The front door slammed and Signor Pino marched out carrying a brown paper bag tucked under his arm. The bulldog trotted behind him, but stopped, growled and snarled at me. Signor Pino's chunky body stooped and two stubby fingers pinched me.

"Look at all these awful crumbs! Why did you drop those cookies? Who's going to clean up this mess?" he rasped. The *amaretto* crunched under the soles of his charcoal shoes and he stomped down the street. The dog licked the crumbs of my cookies before it wobbled away.

I crouched to pick up the rest of the almond biscuit and I fed a few sparrows chirping around the wooden birdhouse. I filled one of my tiny yogourt containers with water and watched the birds dip their beaks into it to drink.

When I opened the door to get in, a white-tailed squirrel scampered in and hid under the laundry hamper in the kitchen. My mother saw the tamed squirrel as she mopped the floor. She picked up a fistful of peanuts and tossed them at the rodent whose teeth gnawed at everything. She took an empty basket from the cupboard. "Come here, Toffee," she said. "Get in and we'll bring you out where you belong." But the squirrel raced into the storage room and made a mess chewing on a small bag of rice in a corner. My mother yelled and shooed Toffee out of the house and I felt sad.

In the evening, my father didn't return home to eat the watery minestrone my mother prepared for us. He probably ate some spaghetti with his poker friends. My father went out every day to look for a job. When he came home, my mother would ask him for money or food. I would wake up at night and I'd listen to my parents argue until my mother would go to bed. She often wept for a long time and her shoulders shook under the blankets. My father would sleep on the couch after a quarrel and he would skip breakfast when he woke up next day.

A knock startled us that spring morning. My father rushed to the door and let in two dark-haired paramedics. The shorter one sported a nail-thin moustache cutting his narrow face in two. The taller paramedic walked with long strides and his shoes left scuff marks on the linoleum.

My father led them both to the bedroom where they slid my mother onto a stretcher. The two paramedics quickly unfolded a grey blanket to cover her and to keep her warm. They lifted the stretcher and carried her outside to the waiting ambulance parked at the curb.

I gripped my father's wrist and tugged at his sleeve. I couldn't speak, but I didn't want to let him go. The salty taste of tears filled my mouth and I clutched his arm tight. He was my only anchor.

"I want to go with you," I cried.

"You can't now. Maybe later." He bent to kiss me on the forehead.

"Papa . . . Why?" I sobbed. "Why?"

"There isn't enough room in the ambulance."

"Mamma . . . ."

"She'll be all right. We'll take care of her. Stop crying. Go water your mother's geraniums and the pink oleanders in the flowerpots. You're a big girl now. Almost twelve years old."

I nodded and wiped my tears with my right palm. "When will I see you?"

"I'll pick you up later and together we'll go visit your mother." He took my arm and pulled me closer to him. I thought he was going to tell me an important secret as he cocked his head to one side. "I'll make sure she gets well, you'll see. There isn't much of a chance for us here. Uncle Remo needs help with his grocery store. We'll move to an apartment near his business downtown. I'll have a good job and we'll start a new life."

I dried my eyes, but they still felt itchy. They burned with the sting of tears. I hugged my father and kissed him on the cheek. He patted my shoulder.

When I heard the shriek of the siren outside, I wanted to catch a glimpse of the ambulance driving down the road. I felt my heart thump faster as I stared out the window. Only grey clouds covered the sky. The pavement was grey and the ice fog spread in thick grey patches to hide the stucco bungalows across the street. I missed my mother and I felt lonely. I made up my mind to look after the pink oleanders in the earthenware flowerpot and the scarlet geraniums on the windowsill. Turning on the tap, I filled a glass to water the plants. I splashed a few drops on the floor and mopped them up. When I finished watering the potted plants, I went out and searched for Toffee near the bird-house, but I couldn't find the tame squirrel anywhere.

My father returned at lunch time. Ashen-faced and still unshaven, he bent over the potted geraniums and he cleaned up a few dry leaves. It was the first time I ever saw him pick up crumbling leaves and take care of the plants. "I can see the new buds sprouting. These geraniums will soon be in full bloom." He put his arm over my shoulders. "Your mother will be proud of you when she finds out how well you've looked after her flowers."

"When is she coming home?"

"In a couple of days, I hope."

"Why can't we pick her up today?"

"She needs more care and some rest." He turned around, stretched out his arm and took a plate from the cupboard. "You can eat a crusty *panino*. Here. Try a slice of this *pagnotta* bread with butter and jam."

"I'm not hungry." I pulled his shirt sleeve. "Can I go with you to the hospital today?"

"We must let your mother rest." My father cut a slice of the crusty *pagnotta* bread and spread some raspberry jam on it. "You'd better eat, or you won't be strong enough to go visit her."

"Si." I chewed on my slice of *pagnotta*, but I couldn't swallow a single bite.

I went into the bedroom and straightened the blankets on my mother's bed. From the top of the night table, I picked up the snifter and brought it back to the kitchen.

"Wait a minute! Let me see that snifter." My father stepped closer to me and snatched the pear-shaped glass from my hands. He raised it to his nose. "Hmmmmh! Smells familiar. Awful! What's that dreadful stink?"

"Signor Pino's *grappa*," I whispered.

"Pino! His *grappa's* terrible." My father put down the glass and stared at me. "Did you see him around?"

I bowed my head. "I saw him yesterday. He was here with Butch, his bulldog."

"Butch! Your mother is allergic to that dog's hair!" My father shook his head. "I warned the landlord not to bring that bulldog here. It bites people. He doesn't listen to me. He couldn't care less if your mother gets sick."

"He was yelling about the rent. Mamma cried when he took . . . ."

"What did he take? Tell me!" My father's face crimsoned. "What?"

"La *zuccheriera d'argento*, the silver sugar bowl set."

"That crook. That pickpocket. Stole our best silver. . . when I wasn't looking. I wasn't home and I couldn't stop him! He charges too much rent and he picks our pockets clean. It's bad. *Brutto mondo*. We won't see that sugar bowl

set ever again. Can't afford to buy another one. It was the
gift I gave to your mother for our first anniversary. That was
your grandmother's." My father shoved the snifter between
the jar of raspberry jam and the *pagnotta*. "Now, I see." He
lifted the pear-shaped glass again and stared at the faint
amber stain at the bottom. He sighed. "I understand."

"What is it?"

"I should have stayed home with you and your mother.
She was homesick and lonely for the friends she left back at
her village. I had to go look for work. Why didn't I understand she needed to talk to someone? Maybe this wouldn't
have happened if I had a job. I'll work harder, you'll see."

"Si! Papa."

"It was a bad mix. Valerian works on her heart. Your
mother insists on taking it. It may be the kind of herb that
doesn't go well with alcohol and the pills she gulps down
every night! I think the landlord brought over some of his
bad tasting *grappa* yesterday on purpose and Lucia took a
couple of caplets too . . . Is that right? All that stuff made
her sick. What a mess. Worse than poison!"

My face felt scorched. "Poison?" I burst into tears.

"Don't cry." My father took my arm.

"Mamma's poisoned?"

"No. No." My father paced the room. "The doctor will
take care of your mother. He'll wash her stomach and flush
out the poison from her system. She'll be fine." He stopped
beside me and took my hand. "We'll go visit her later this
afternoon."

My father went into the living room and I followed
him. He pulled out three drawers of the hutch and slammed
them shut.

"Papa . . . What are you looking for?"

"The keys for the big trunk and our two suitcases. Have

you seen them around? They're silver with a square crest on top."

"Mamma used them yesterday and put them away in the kitchen drawer." I licked the jam and bit into the bread. I cupped my hand underneath my chin to make sure I would not drop any crumbs on the floor.

My father tapped my shoulder. "That's my girl. We'll find the keys and we'll get ready to pack."

"Mamma's coming with us, isn't she?" The crust was too salty to eat for me and I wanted to spit it out, but I didn't dare.

"Sure, she is. Your mother will be home soon and we'll move. We'll be together. The three of us." He rushed to search for the keys in the kitchen. "Here's what we need." The keys clinked in his hands.

"Let me see. One. Two." I counted them. "Only two?"

My father shook the keys. "That's all I could find for now." The keys rattled.

I swallowed the wrong way and coughed. "Where's the third one? Why don't I have my own key?" I lifted my chin. "Can't I go with you?"

"Sure." My father pulled me closer. "You're part of my family, aren't you?" As he opened the door of the storage room, it squeaked on its hinges. I expected to find Toffee chewing at the rice again. "There's our old suitcase. The big grey *valigia*. See? You're sharing this suitcase with me. We'll move in together and we'll take care of your mother."

I pursed my lips. "Si." I believed my father, but I didn't know how long it would take for my mother to get well and to return from the hospital.

Would she be able to water her pink oleanders or to make my hot chocolate ever again? When would she feel well enough to move to a new apartment with us? I watered again the potted geraniums on the windowsill and I pruned a few leaves.

I sat down with my books and I finished eating my slice of *pagnotta* bread.

I was anxious to go visit my mother that afternoon. I knew she needed a big hug, but we would have to wait. I looked out of the window. My eyes felt itchy and I rubbed them hard.

I turned around.

I didn't want to see the grey clouds in the sky.

CLOSE CALL

Didn't want to get up too early. Six o'clock. The usual grind. I stretched out my arms. Couldn't feel the warmth of Bren's body beside me. The bedspread was rolled up on his side and his pillow stood propped up against the bed rest. Never heard him coming home last night. Must have been very late.

I swung my legs over the ruffled bed skirt, grabbed my jeans and drew back the cocoa curtains. The blush of dawn tinged the horizon with purple, but chains of dark clouds threatened pouring rain.

Venturing silently along the corridor, I peered into the children's room. They were both still asleep. Two little angels, cherubs with rosy round cheeks. Didn't want to wake them up and I tiptoed past their door. Needed some peace and quiet around the house until I'd drink my coffee and wake up a bit.

Smells of toast and fried bacon spread in waves from the kitchen where I found Bren standing near the stove. He was poking narrow strips of bacon with his fork and he tossed a few more into the sizzling grease of the frying pan. The bacon curled into browned ripples and coils. The melting fat crackled, spraying all around the burner and showering the nearby wall.

"Careful," I said.

He grinned. "Surprised, huh?" He shoved some of the bacon curls to one side of the frying pan and broke the shells of two eggs as if he were having fun. "Didn't even know I could cook, right?" His hair was so short, he didn't even have to comb it when he got up. He would need a shave though. "You'll have to try the breakfast I'm making. Then, you'll know what good food tastes like."

"Trying to make up for coming home late last night?"

"Just wanted to have a bite to eat. Must work in the yard before it rains. It's hot and muggy."

"Why were you late? Went to the casino and lost some hard-earned cash?"

"It was Friday night. Stormy had a big fight with his girlfriend. Threatened to cut his wrists and hers. Had to get him out of the house. He needed someone to talk to."

"Sounds bad." I sighed. "You sure he's not going to do her in?"

"You mean Roselynn?" He forked out some bacon and placed it in a plate. "She lives nearby. She'll be all right."

"If you say so." I munched on a crispy curl of bacon. On Saturday, I felt better thinking he would stay around and help me look after the children. They enjoyed playing in the backyard, but they needed strict supervision or they would put themselves in trouble. At times, if I didn't watch them, they would both run crying to me for a bandage after falling and scraping the skin off their foreheads on the gravel path near the sandbox.

Bren fished out more of the curled-up bacon from the grease bubbling in the frying pan. He placed the rippled strips across the plate and added a fried egg beside them.

"How do you like your toast?" he asked me.

"Brown. But don't burn it."

The toaster clicked as the toast popped up. It was kind

of crusty, but became chewy when I spread a sliver of butter on top.

Bren stuffed a bacon strip into his mouth, took a bite out of his toast and gulped down a glass of milk. "Have to rush out before the children wake up."

"Shh! Not so loud." I had to stop myself from complaining about cleaning up the mess every day.

"Mowing the lawn with them close by becomes next to impossible."

"Have you heard about that child who tried his father's lawnmower when it was left with the motor running?"

"Guess not." Bren shaved off a sliver of butter for his toast. "What about that?"

"The child was too little. Couldn't handle the mower. Cut his own toes."

"Frightful."

Bren finished his toast and swallowed more milk. He waved to me and hurried out of the kitchen. But as he took his sand cap from a hook, Darryl, our two-year-old, wobbled across the hallway. His chubby little hands reached for Bren's leg.

"Dadaaaa . . ." He tugged at his father's bluejeans.

Bren patted the blond fuzz that grew sticking out on both sides of his little head. "Want to come out later and play in the sandbox?"

"Yaaahh!" He glanced up and clutched his tiny white runners. He looked eager to put them on and to go explore everything outside.

More steps could be heard in the hallway. Still in his pajamas, Darrin, our five-year-old, was driving his red fire engine along the hallway. His brown curls framed his round face and a couple of them fell down to his eyes.

"Beeeeep! Beep, beep!" he shouted. "Out of the way."

The shiny toy truck rolled along the linoleum floor and bumped against Darryl's sturdy legs with a thud. "Ouch! Ouuchhh!" the tot cried out, his baby face reddening. Tears swelled in his eyes as he twisted around and grasped the metal ladder of the fire engine.

"Hey! That's mine." Darrin shoved his younger brother aside and took over driving his toy truck along the wall.

"No!" Darryl sobbed. He threw himself onto the toy truck and Darrin attacked him from behind.

Bren bent over and picked up little Darryl. "We'll buy another toy fire engine for you. A yellow one."

"Yahhh! Nowww."

"Not now. Have to go out and cut the lawn." Bren put down the toddler who clutched his ankle tight and would not let go.

"Daaad . . ." Darryl shouted, squirming at his feet.

"You'll come out with me later."

"Want to come too," Darrin cried out.

"You both have to eat your breakfast first." Bren patted the blond fuzz on Darryl's head. "Go with your Mummy."

"Awright," I said, taking Darryl's wrist. "Let's go in the kitchen."

"Noooo!" Darryl screamed, kicking the wall.

I stroked his rosy red cheeks. "We'll feed Chinsing."

Darrin grabbed his fire engine. "Vrooomm. Vroom."

We headed for the kitchen and Bren left. Darrin parked his miniature fire engine near the leg of the table.

"Chinsing!" Darrin called out to the white and orange striped kitten curled up in a corner.

Chinsing stretched, arching its little body and yawning. Darryl giggled and reached for the kitten's tail, but Darrin picked up Chinsing. He petted the furry kitten that clawed at the scarlet ball of yarn peeking out of a sewing basket.

The yarn unrolled itself and Chinsing scuttled across the kitchen floor to the hallway leading to the exit.

"Chinsing doesn't want to eat his breakfast!" Darrin shouted.

"Bad," Darryl echoed.

"Like you, duh!" Darrin smacked his lips.

I scooped up some dry porridge, mixed it with a cup of boiling water, stirred it and got rid of all the lumps until the texture became smooth and creamy. I poured the porridge into two bowls, sprinkled a pinch of brown sugar on top and added some milk to cool it down.

"Try your porridge," I said, serving them.

Darrin dipped his teaspoon into the steaming hot porridge. The mixture was so thick that the spoon stood like a spout sculptured in the middle of the bowl. "It's too hot." He blew over his hot cereal and tasted it, but dropped his spoon spilling some porridge on the table.

"Be careful. Porridge sticks like glue. Hard to clean." I started wiping the table with a wet cloth. But, Chinsing returned in the kitchen, jumped onto the table and made the imprints of its paws on the spilled porridge. It looked like someone stepping on the soft, freshly poured cement of a sidewalk. "Get down," I said, and Chinsing hopped to the floor, leaving more paw imprints.

"Don't want porridge." Darrin pushed his bowl aside.

"Fine, I'll make some toast." The children always liked to hear the toaster click as the two brown slices of toast popped out. "Here's your toast with jam and butter." I gave the first one to Darryl who tore apart his toast as if he wanted to see what might be inside. As he took a bite, he smeared his face with raspberry jam.

Darrin licked the crust of his toast. He turned away. "Tastes burnt," he whimpered.

"You haven't even touched your toast," I said. "How do you know what it tastes like?"

"Smells funny!" He pointed to his little brother. "Darryl has blood on his face. Ahahh!"

Darryl touched the red jam on his cheek and painted a crooked moustache under his nose. He giggled and Darrin pommelled the metal cover of the jam jar as if it were a kettledrum. Darryl stuffed a piece of toast into his mouth and joined his older brother in beating the lid of the jar.

Darrin strained against the table and stretched out his hand. He grabbed a cinnamon bun from the metal tray by the toaster. But Darryl snatched the bun away and dropped it on the floor. They both rushed to fetch the cinnamon bun, bumping into each other like two football players.

"Mine!" Darryl yelled.

"No, it's not," his brother screamed, but he couldn't pick it up. The sugary bun was glued to the linoleum.

"You're still in your jamas," I said. "Let's go wash up and dress."

They both rushed to wash their hands. I waited for them in the bedroom. Darrin would choose his clothes each day and he would comb his hair with a wet brush to tame his curls. He believed he should decide which way his hair could go, but his curls had a mind of their own. The last time I cut his hair, I had to go answer the phone. Darrin took the scissors and snipped off some of Darryl's fuzz. I got mad at both of them, but couldn't punish them.

"Mummy!" Darrin cried. "Just wanted to help you with Darryl."

I put away the scissors and couldn't resist giving them a bear hug. "You're all heart!" I smiled at Darrin.

It was already eight o'clock when we heard our lawn-mower roar outside, but it stalled.

"Can I go out?" Darrin asked me after he put on his burnt-orange shirt and navy blue shorts.

"You're old enough to understand you must stay away from the lawnmower," I warned him.

He nodded and rushed out as I helped Darryl change into his T-shirt with a brown bear's paw painted in front.

"Wanna go out too." Darryl headed for the door.

"Wait for me," I said. "I'll change my sneakers and we'll go out together."

Darryl climbed onto the couch next to the large picture window overlooking our yard. He pursed his lips and pointed outside. "Wanna go with Darrin."

"I guess in a few minutes!" I insisted. "Daddy's mowing the lawn. But wait a sec. Can't hear the lawnmower."

I strolled into my bedroom and picked up my Caravaggio peach print dress. It felt softer than the acid-washed bluejeans I was wearing. As I took off the jeans, a loud shriek scared me. I froze and listened.

"Maaaa!" Darryl yelled. He never screamed like that before. Was he hurt? "Mummy!" His voice, a terrified shrill. The pitch of his scream was higher than the day when his little finger got caught in the folding doors of the closet and was pinched so hard it bled.

I shuddered. Didn't want to see him hurt. I could hear him hammering at the picture window. If he broke the windowpane, the glass would cut his face and throat. What could be bothering him so much? I was afraid to find out. Whatever it was, I would have to face it.

With shaky hands, I pulled my bluejeans back on and ran into the living room. Darryl was pounding the glass of the window with both fists.

"Watch out. You're going to break the glass."

He widened his eyes in terror. "Maaa!" He sobbed.

"I'm here with you. There's nothing to worry about." I tried to pick him up and cuddle him in my arms, but he drew back from me and pounded harder on the window-pane. "What's the trouble?"

He tugged at my T-shirt and cried out, "Fire. Fire. In the garage. And Darrin is inside." He gasped. "Can't get out." He burst into tears.

I jumped up and stared outside. Horror. Orange flames shot up at the entrance of the garage, long tongues licking at the roof. Where was Bren? He was nowhere in sight. And Darrin? How could he be trapped inside the garage? Wouldn't Bren be with him? I couldn't see anything else but the hypnotic glow of the fire spreading fast to the grass. If I didn't hurry, I would have to go through hell to get my boy out of the garage.

Ran out barefoot. The flames were lapping at the south wall of the garage. The scorching heat and black smoke made my throat feel dry and sore. I coughed. The thickening smoke was stinging my eyes. The smell of burnt grass sickened me, but I pulled my shirt over my nose and mouth as I rushed through the black curtain of smoke. Couldn't find Darrin. Too much smoke.

Our blue Chev seemed to have turned a ghostly grey as if covered with layers of dust. Couldn't see the shelves at the rear of the garage. I stumbled on a piece of wood. I could barely make out in a corner the big box full of old toys. Darrin stood there dazed, holding a one-eared stuffed bear to his chest. He looked bewildered. Hypnotized. In awe. Amazed rather than terrified. I took him in my arms.

"Get out of here! Both of you. Hurry." Bren rushed past us. He fumbled in the corner where the fire extinguisher was wedged between an old tire and a roll of rusty wire.

With Darrin, I ran out of the smoke-filled garage. Bren

sprayed the wall near the entrance to stop the fire from spreading. His red fire extinguisher sprayed, foamed and hissed, smothering the flames with a jet of whitish powder.

Darrin was still squeezing his stuffed bear to his chest as I dragged the garden hose toward the garage to help put out the fire. Blades of grass were smoldering along the wall. The strong jet of water shooting out from the hose made my hands shake, as if I were holding a live snake. With one last crackle, the flames sighed and died.

A siren wailed down the street. A bright yellow fire truck screeched to a halt in front of our house. A stocky firefighter jumped down, leaving his companion in charge of the truck. Taking long steps in his yellow rubber boots, he headed toward us.

"Having trouble?" The firefighter glared at us. It was Stormy, wearing his yellow helmet and an olive green canvas jacket with matching ribbed gloves.

His face caked with sweat and dust, Bren rushed to him. "Sure glad to see you, Stormy."

"Roselynn called us." Stormy waved his gloved hand. "Saw the smoke."

Bren shook his head. "Scared, I guess."

"The grass is burnt near the garage." Stormy stomped in front of the blackened entrance. "You'll have to replace the door and the frame."

Bren bowed his head. "Yeah!"

"That will keep you busy. Out of trouble." Stormy took off his gloves and tucked them under his arm. He frowned, pulled out a pen and jotted down a few lines on his notebook. "Have to report this."

"The lawnmower gave me trouble." Bren wanted to explain what happened, even though he didn't know why. "The tank was empty. Had to pour in some gas. But that curious kitten jumped on top of the gas can and knocked it over." Bren wiped the sweat and dust from his brow and motioned at Chinsing pouncing through the tall grass.

"That cute kitten?" Stormy noticed Chinsing scampering behind a ceramic flowerpot as Darryl gave chase. "Hah! That furry little orange ball?"

Bren picked up what looked like a charred stick. "Look at this. Burnt black. It's all I have left of my lighter."

"Which lighter?" Stormy looked puzzled, but he jotted down a few more words. "What does the kitten have to do with your lighter?"

"Gas was gurgling out of the overturned can. As I bent over to pick up the can, the lighter fell out of my shirt pocket. A spark flew through the air. It ignited the gas. Flames shot up pretty high." Bren gestured to an overturned plastic pail abandoned nearby. "Fetched some sand from the sandbox. I wanted to smother the fire, but it was getting out of hand. Darrin was still in the garage. Didn't know what to do. I went back in and found our fire extinguisher."

"Good thing you had it working for you." Stormy scribbled another line in his notebook. "But with kids and kittens around, you have to watch what you're doing," he warned Bren, as if he knew what was best for him. "Got to watch those adults too. Our girlfriends. Or wives."

Bren pointed at me. "Had Sarah not helped me hose down those flames, the garage would have burned to the ground. And she got Darrin out."

"That was close. I know the feeling." Stormy patted Darrin's curls and headed back to his fire truck.

"Sure was a close call."

Darryl chased after Chinsing until he bumped into my shin and giggled. He clutched my knee and wouldn't let go. I picked him up. He gripped my neck and pulled my hair as the fire engine left with a roar.

"Wanna that big fire truck." Darryl pointed down the street. "Mummy. That one!"

I held him tighter in my arms. "Not like Stormy's fire truck. You'd be better off to have your own. Not someone else's."

"Wanna that fire truck. Wanna now!"

He pursed his lips and tugged harder on my hair, but I'm glad he didn't cry.

CLIFF

Cliff didn't want to bother talking to Sheena after that night in May when they had a fight and he beat her black and blue. She begged him to stop. But he pushed her down the front steps and she hurt her elbow.

He went out as usual. He would spend hours playing the video lottery at the Rham Hotel downtown. Cliff worked as a computer technician and he believed he could make machines and people do what he wanted. He didn't show up at work when he gambled and lost all his money. He would drink. His job was in jeopardy and he was afraid Sheena would leave him. But she couldn't stay with him.

She ran away. She planned to hitchhike down south.

Her leather-collared windbreaker made her look neat, but she had a black eye and a violet-shaped bruise surfacing from underneath her melon-and-peach makeup.

A mud-covered car halted on the shoulder of the road when she stuck out her thumb for a ride. She quickly got into the car. The driver's face was hidden by a large-rimmed cowboy hat and his ponytail swung when they took off and turned onto a rutted country road. It was rough driving. Sheena pressed her lips tight and hung on for dear life.

He slowed down by a grove of elm trees and grabbed the sleeve of her windbreaker. She slid her arms out of the sleeves and left the garment in the driver's hands. He tossed the windbreaker onto the back seat.

She threw herself out of the moving car and raced to the cluster of elm trees. The brakes squealed and the man yelled, "Heh!" He chased her, but he stumbled. Thorny bushes caught his ponytail and ripped his shirt.

Sheena kept running, but lost one of her shoes when her foot sank into a puddle. Mud splashed her, tattooing her jeans and blouse. She felt cold and wet without her windbreaker.

Her bluejeans were torn, and her legs scratched. She headed for a pitch-roofed building silhouetted against the sky in the distance. It was much further than she thought.

As she approached, she noticed the log building wasn't just one cabin. It was a row of cabins and a name flickered on top of the office roof, *Nite Snooze Inn.*

She slipped past the office and walked to the nearest brown log cabin. She found the door unlocked. She pushed it open and went in. She shut the door with a sigh of relief.

A double bed stood in the middle of the room and a sepia bedspread was folded over it, as if someone was getting ready to lie down. But there was no one around. Sheena felt at home. She would wash her jeans and warm up her cold feet in the shower.

Sheena strolled into the bathroom, but her foot slid on the wet tiles in front of the sink and she banged her head against the edge of the mirrored cabinet.

I found her lying sprawled on the bathroom floor when I went in to hang up clean towels and a new shower mat. I was puzzled. Concerned. She might be one of the guests and I didn't want any trouble.

I knelt beside her and slipped a folded towel under her head. As I dabbed her temples with a damp facecloth, her eyelids quivered. "Are you hurt?"

"Where am I?" she murmured.

"At the *Nite Snooze Inn*," I replied.

"Awwright! A great night. Don't let the bugs bite." She stood up and took a few steps. She glanced at the dust streaming within the sun's rays bursting through the window. "Too bad it's not night, now!" She sighed.

"It's daytime. Almost noon. Check-out time!"

"Why am I here?"

"Dunno! Maybe you forgot something here," I said. I thought she was a bit confused.

"Looks like I forgot everything." She slapped her forehead and stared at me as if it were my fault.

"You had a rough time. Right?"

"Not so sure I want to find out." She fingered the violet bruise on her face.

"Don't you have a purse? A wallet?"

"No. Guess I lost it. Who are you?"

"I'm Sarah. I work here."

"Can you find out where I live?" She stared past me and glanced around. "I bet I live not too far from here."

I led her across the room. "Let's find out if you're on the guest list. Your address should be there. Your memory will come back to you." I came to an abrupt halt. "But I'd need your name."

She walked out. "Have to think about that."

I brought her to the office and gave her some green tea. She couldn't recognize any of the names on the list of the registered guests. She still didn't seem to recall where she lived and who she was. But she stared intently at the television news about winning the weekly jackpot.

After a new brown Bronco screeched to a stop in front of the office, a man walked in and grinned. Sturdy-built, he stood there at the entrance, perspiring and fidgeting with his belt buckle. Sheena crouched behind the desk.

"What can I do for you?" I said.

"Don't know yet. I have to talk to Sheena first," he replied, waving to her.

Sheena widened her eyes and grimaced. "Cliff?"

"I've changed my car. See?" He stuck his thumb toward his Bronco parked outside. "I've hit the jackpot!"

"Cliff?" She cocked her head to one side and her hair became a dark fan resembling the wing of a raven in flight. She stormed out of the office and darted across the yard into the bushes growing thick next to the motel.

"Sheena!" he screamed.

Stretching out my arm, I tried to block Cliff's path. If I could make him stay longer with me in the office, Sheena might have a better chance to flee.

"Get out of the way!" He shoved me against the wall.

I tripped on the rug and tried to grab his shirt, but I couldn't stop him. He rushed out and started the engine of his Bronco.

I took a deep breath and dialed 911.

I haven't heard anything else from Sheena, but I think the Bronco could not drive through the thick underbrush nearby. Maybe she got away.

A man from New York rented a room today. He insists he met Sheena. She might be hiding somewhere out there. Either in the city or in the wilderness. I can't blame her for forgetting her past. But now at least she knows what her name is.

CAMPING AT LAKE WABAMUN

Milky-white streaks of cirrus tendrils swelled into monster tentacles spreading out to reach the horizon. Highway 16 stretched its grey-speckled tongue in the distance ahead.

It was windy and streamers of lightning galvanized the sky. Thunder grumbled as a spring storm menaced the city. I did not want to be caught in the rain and I pressed down harder on the gas pedal.

The engine sputtered and the yolk-yellow hood shook as my Toyota picked up speed. I had never been to Lake Wabamun and I was worried about missing the right turn to get to the camp, but I was in too much of a hurry to slow down and pay attention to the signs.

I wanted to surprise Darrin. He went camping with his friends and couldn't stuff everything into his backpack. I would deliver the gear I just bought for him.

When Darrin came home from school three days ago, he hung his coat in the closet. He didn't pick up a can of pop in the fridge. Strange. He remained in his room and cleaned out his desk. Quite unusual.

I stood at the doorway and watched him. He scratched his head. He pulled out a green sheet from his binder and handed it to me. It was a brief notice about an upcoming camping trip. Darrin had never gone camping before. That would be a unique experience to share with his best friends. They would leave early on Friday morning for Camp Yoo-Hoo-Haw where they would have a sleep over, wiener roasts and nature walks on an unspoiled stretch of beach along Lake Wabamun, away from pollution and noise.

I knew I would miss him, but if I wouldn't let him go camping, he would take that as a form of punishment he didn't deserve. He would feel left out. He was very excited about spending the long weekend away from home and I couldn't change his plans. He wanted to explore nature, to try out canoeing or kayaking and maybe even to learn a few tips about how to survive in the wilderness. Boys and girls in grade seven would camp out in their separate tents for the weekend. I would have liked to go along, but chose not to bother the group. I didn't want to butt in and spoil Darrin's camping trip.

On Thursday evening, Darrin set his blue duffel bag on his bed and started packing. He rolled up a brand new pair of bluejeans and stuffed them inside the duffel bag with two cotton T-shirts, two pullovers, six pairs of socks, underwears and clamdiggers. I didn't mind helping him pack and I wrapped his new pair of sneakers next to his black rubber boots. I took his biscuit coloured jacket from the hanger in the closet and slid his raincoat out of a drawer. But when I grabbed his flannelette pyjamas, he stepped closer to me.

"Don't need that," he said and snatched the striped pyjamas from my hands. He tossed it back into the drawer. His face was losing its peach fuzz, but he still had the boyish look that always led me to expect a prank from him. He combed his short hair to one side and left a long strand growing like a tail at the back of his head.

"What's wrong, Darrin?" I asked him.

"Those jamas have stripes. Make me look funny. Like I

wear some kind of prison garb."

"Who's going to look at you at night?"

He reddened as if I had slapped him on both cheeks. "No one . . . Never mind." He fumbled into the drawer and pulled out his plain blue cotton pyjamas. "These will do."

"Bet girls like Maureen are even more worried than you are about what to wear," I said.

"Aww . . . right!"

"But why should we worry about what they wear?" I joked.

He glanced away and stepped back, shoving a chair against his dresser. His long strand of brown hair swept his shoulders. With his fists, he squeezed all his clothes inside his duffel bag and closed it. "Hmmphh!" He tried to lift the bag onto the chair.

"Don't know why you have to bring along all these clothes. It's just a weekend at the lake, for heaven's sake. What will you jam in there next? Pack the computer, keyboard with monitor, and plant them in the woods?"

"Mum . . . awww! Don't get mad at me."

"Boy, have I got news for you!" I glared at him. "You forgot the most important item on your list."

"And what's that?" He widened his eyes, the pupils brown like two ripe hazelnuts.

"A sleeping bag."

He smacked his forehead with his hand and frowned. "Don't have a sleeping bag." He groped into his closet and shrugged. "Never went camping before."

"Guess what? You can sleep on the bare ground or up on a tree." I teased him.

He shook his head and bit the broken nail on his middle finger. "I could start delivering papers to buy my sleeping bag. What do you think?"

"You'd need more time to earn something. We'll find a way and work things out." I couldn't purchase the sleeping bag unless I used my credit card or paid the bill later on. I would have to work overtime, but it might just be worth the effort. "I'll buy the sleeping bag for you."

"Aww . . . right!" He touched my arm. "Don't need to go shopping with you, do I?"

"It's too late to shop now. Tomorrow after work, I'll look around everywhere to find the best sleeping bag in the city," I boasted.

"But I'll leave early tomorrow morning on the school bus." Darrin sighed. "How can I get my sleeping bag?"

"I'll deliver it to you tomorrow night."

"You're not going to stay overnight, are you?" He stared at me with apprehension.

"No way. I've got plenty of work to do around here." I walked to the door.

"Maybe I'll bring home a pet for you." He grinned.

I understood Darrin wanted to have a pet, but I was not sure if we had enough room. "Who's going to take care of the feeding and cleaning?"

"Mum!" He put one hand over his mouth and laughed. "Right?"

"We could look after it together. But I'm too busy." I strolled down the hallway. "Have to run. I've something in the oven." The sweet fragrance of the apple pie I was baking spread through the air. It smelled like fruity cinnamon.

Darrin whistled. "Hmmmm! What's cooking?"

"Your favourite. Apple pie."

"Can I have some?"

"Sure. I'll add two scoops of ice cream."

"Neat-oh!" He threw his arms around my neck and gave me a bear hug.

He followed me into the kitchen, opened the fridge and poured himself a glass of Coke. It fizzed out of the can. He laughed. "It tickles my nose."

I took the hot apple pie from the oven and cut a big slice for Darrin. "Watch out. It's still too hot."

He poked at the sugary crust and tasted the syrupy filling. "Hmmmmm!"

"Don't burn your tongue. Wait . . . Leave it cool off for a couple of minutes."

"It's too good to wait."

My Toyota bounced along the highway as I pumped the gas pedal. Gusts of wind blew stronger. I looked farther down the road and I saw the slim silhouette of a girl standing on the shoulder of the road. She was hitchhiking. She stretched out one arm to flag down my car. As I slowed down and pulled over, I noticed the frame of a bicycle leaning against the bulky shapes of a knapsack and sleeping bag.

"Need any help?" I asked.

The hitchhiker bent over to reach for the window on the passenger side. "My bike got a flat tire." She pointed to the front wheel of her bicycle. "See?"

"I can find some room in my trunk. Where are you heading?"

"To Camp Yoo-Hoo-Haw," she said. A wind gust blew a long bang of blond hair over her eyebrows. With her bony fingers, she pushed back her hair. A few freckles dotted her nose and cheeks.

"I'm heading that way too." I got out and went to unlock the trunk. The hitchhiker brought her bike and her canvas knapsack closer to my car. We put them inside the trunk and added the two brown bags of groceries she had carried in the basket clamped to the front of her bike.

"There," she said and sat beside me on the front seat. "I'm Maureen. Good thing you've stopped for me. Or my friends would have been waiting for a long time for their wiener roast tonight. I'm in charge of bringing more buns, ketchup, relish and mustard."

So, I get to talk to Maureen. "Been there before?"

"No. But we can follow the signs." She gazed out of the window and sighed. "We might have to turn at the next intersection."

"Why didn't you leave earlier with your friends?"

"Had to work at the *Periwinkle*." Maureen glanced at me. Her skin was honey-smooth. When she smiled, she had dimples on her cheeks that made her look younger, even though she might be old enough to be in grade eleven. "Do you know where that is?"

"I've heard about that. It's a new trendy restaurant at the edge of town."

"Yeah!" She nodded. "That's why I'm bringing the food. They gave it to me as a bonus for washing dishes."

"Nice of you to share."

"Let's hope it doesn't rain." Maureen stared at the sky.

"It might shower," I said.

On the right shoulder of the highway, a bright green sign stood tall boasting an arrow pointing in the direction of Lake Wabamun. I sped up toward the next crossing and I glanced in the rearview mirror. I wanted to change lanes and turn left when I saw a police cruiser parked at the exit of a service road. It had the red and blue lights flashing on top like eyes watching us. A giant, uniformed policeman stepped out and waved to me.

"Is this a speed trap?" I took a deep breath. I wanted to press down harder on the gas to speed away, but I pulled to the right. My car squeaked to a halt.

The officer approached. He tapped at my window. Under his blue cap, his clean shaven face became serious.

"Can I see your registration and your driver's license?" He scowled.

"Sure." I slid the pink card and my license out of my wallet. "Here they are."

The officer examined my documents. "You were speeding. Five kilometres over the speed limit." He frowned.

I stared at the speedometer in disbelief. "I . . . I didn't know."

"That doesn't let you off the hook," he scolded me. "You should keep your eyes open and watch your speed."

Maureen glanced at me. "It's my fault. I shouldn't have distracted the driver."

"Talking away, hah?" The policeman shook his head in disapproval. "Not paying too much attention."

"She stopped to give me a ride, or I might still be back there . . . hitchhiking."

"Hitchhiking, ah?" The officer scowled. "That's not the best way of travelling, especially for a young lady."

"I tried to bike to Camp Yoo-Hoo-Haw, but I got a flat tire," Maureen said.

"We're both heading to the lake," I intervened. "She's bringing food supplies and I have some camping gear to deliver to my son. Can you tell us how to get there?"

The officer twisted around and stretched out his arm. "Turn left at the first intersection and follow the gravel road. At the next crossing, you'll have to go left again for at least a hundred metres." The constable raised his hand. "Stay on the road and you'll arrive at the camp."

"Is there a sign?" I asked him.

"A small one. You will recognize the place for sure. It's kind of a rustic site, surrounded by spruce trees."

"Sounds great to me." I nodded.

"It's not bad. But when it rains, you'll have mud up to your knees." The policeman glanced at the lead sky. "Looks like we might get some rain tonight."

I didn't want to let him know I was in a hurry. "Hope to reach the camp before it starts raining," I said.

I remembered when I went camping on a long weekend one summer. It was my first field trip and we were all girls. We camped on a strip of sand snaking among the rocks leading to an emerald lake nested in the mountains. A storm of hail and icy cold rain interrupted our fun. We took shelter in an abandoned cabin which had bare walls, a wooden table and a bench. We couldn't go swimming or boating that afternoon. Too wet. Freezing.

By supper time, we managed to dig up a few dry twigs to start a campfire. We sang sitting around the campfire to keep warm. One of my friends strolled through the bushes nearby to gather ripe saskatoons and I caught up to her. We ate some ripe berries until our mouths became purple-blue, but we stopped eating when we saw a snake slither through the wet grass. Shining like a string of green and yellow beads, the reptile slithered closer to my feet. My shoes were stuck in the mud. I couldn't move. I froze. Couldn't scream. My heart pummeled. Jerking her body back, my friend grabbed my elbow and pulled me away.

We ran to join the rest of the girls and I told them about the snake. No one wanted to sleep in the tent that evening. We spent the night huddled inside the log cabin and took turns watching for snakes crawling in.

The policeman gave me back my license with the pink registration slip. "This time, I'm giving you only a warning.

I know it's Friday night, but you must be careful. Don't want trouble or a speeding ticket, do you?"

I bowed my head. "Right. I'll watch my speed."

The officer strolled back to his cruiser and switched off the flashing lights.

I turned the key in the ignition, started my Toyota, put it in gear and followed the instructions the officer gave us.

We reached the camp near a blue-grey lake under a stormy sky. I was glad to see Darrin among his peers. Sitting among their teachers in jeans and T-shirts, the kids were cooking hot-dogs on blackened sticks. The smell of onions and roasted wieners wafted through the air and made me hungry. But they ran out of buns. Maureen smiled, a dimple digging into each one of her cheeks. Like a magician doing a trick, she took out the buns and the jars of mustard and relish from the two brown bags she had brought along.

Darrin stood beside her. A bit shorter, he didn't seem to mind talking to the girl. He offered me a hot dog and prepared one more for Maureen. She took it, bit into the bun, chewed and swallowed.

Darrin bent over, checking her bike. He wanted to fix the flat tire, but a furry rabbit darted out from the shrubs close by and hopped into a cluster of red cedars. Darrin jumped up and chased after the grey rabbit.

"Just try and catch that fluffy ball of fur!" Maureen screamed. "You wish you could keep it as a pet. But a cage might not be the best for the rabbit. Let him go!" She put down her hot dog. "Just arrived at the right time. Wild animals show up, either at dawn or at dusk."

Maureen went after Darrin who was racing among the trees. Their screams and the snapping of twigs would scare the rabbit away even further. But after a few minutes, we couldn't hear their voices anymore.

I wanted to go looking for them, but I didn't. I was concerned and I started roasting marshmallows to keep myself busy. *Maybe they will show up soon*, I thought.

Darrin couldn't catch up to the rabbit and Maureen put her arm around his shoulders to console him when they returned to camp.

The storm burst into action whipping us with cold rain and hail. We got soaking wet.

Maureen's long fringe of blond hair fell down to her eyes. I left her my raincoat before driving back to the city.

The hail storm didn't bother me as I drove back safely, without getting a speeding ticket.

Darrin bought himself a pet rabbit to make up for the one he chased into the woods. More lean and agile, Darrin seems to have grown up an inch just in a couple of days. He is not as shy as he used to be. He doesn't complain anymore about driving with me to the shopping centre.

He understands that I am always careful and I have to watch my speed when I drive anywhere in the country or in the city.

Road Rage

"Speed, or sex?" Hubcaps scrape against the curb and a rusty station wagon swerves to avoid a Ford. Skid marks stretch like thick bundles of black snakes on a bare stretch of pavement. "What's it going to be, huh?" The dishevelled driver crimsons, waving his fist out the window.

"Don't want to know." The blue Ford roars and rattles, racing the station wagon.

Kerry Teal, my neighbour, drives too fast. He has a bad temper and I wouldn't want to get him mad. My friend Lindsay sits beside him. She leans toward him and her bronze hair whips his shoulder as the car bolts forward and the drone of the engine melts into a loud sputtering.

"Christ! Watch out. Sex and speed don't go together." The station wagon crosses over the solid yellow line. "Brain dead!" The red-faced motorist sticks his head out and a few of his dark, wiry bristles quiver like feathers. Bulging veins pulsate on his temples. "What do you think you're doing?"

"You don't want to know." Kerry makes his Ford leap ahead as if it were a wild colt. Bang. The engine misfires.

"Heh! It's spring." The rusty station wagon sideswipes Kerry's blue Ford. Crunch.

"Don't make me mad. Or you'll be sorry." Kerry's Ford gasps, grating the side of the station wagon. Fingers tighten around the tan steering wheel and Kerry strokes a copper bracelet circling his wrist like a handcuff.

A hairy fist rams the side of his vehicle as the driver of the swerving station wagon honks his horn. "Get you later." He speeds up and runs a red light, but screeches to a halt when a semitrailer cuts across his lane.

Kerry squeals past the traffic light too. Lindsay bumps her head against the roof of the car and pulls her hair back.

"We'll try to catch him." Kerry speeds up to the station wagon. "There." He draws Lindsay closer to him.

Veins on the temples of the driver of the station wagon swell and he rolls his eyes around as if they are about to pop. "Have to call the police," he shouts at the blue Ford.

Kerry laughs. With a clank, his Ford lurches ahead, its front wheel flattening a sand bag on the road.

The purple veins surge in a crimson wave of rage. The station wagon rattles to a halt. A hand pulls out a knife. The blade scrapes past the window, hits Kerry's bracelet and stabs at the dashboard of his Ford.

Kerry grabs the handle and flings the knife to the pavement. The rusty station wagon waits as the Ford veers and brakes to a stop.

The driver gets out of his station wagon. He brandishes a wrench high above his head and he stomps closer to Kerry who wriggles out of his car seat. He swings his arm forward and snatches the wrench out of the threatening motorist's hand. Their arms lock together in a wrestlers' struggle. Both their faces become flushed and the tattoo of a naked girl bulges on Kerry's biceps. With a powerful punch to the jaw, Kerry knocks his opponent to the ground.

I lean against the steering wheel and hit my horn. The other motorists around me join in, startling the two men fighting in a slushy puddle in the middle of the road.

Kerry stands up. He looks around, his eyes bloodshot.

The other driver rubs off some mud from his pants and he trudges back to his station wagon. Holding on to the steering wheel, the man pushes his vehicle, steering it nearer to the curb.

Lindsay waves to me as I drive past her to go home.

Later, she storms into my room before I shut the door.

"Kerry watches over his blue Ford like a hawk. He is ready to fight anyone who bothers him," Lindsay warns me.

"So I noticed." I think of bad tempered Khoren.

"That bloody motorist waited for him to get out of his car, then he attacked him." Her voice booms, like a worn tape about to snap.

"Did Kerry ever get mad!"

Lindsay shrugs. When she slumps down onto her small single bed, the springs creak like they were going to break. She is all eyes, and big bones. Her hair has strawberry tips. Her face is tanned. Her wind-burnt nose is peeling.

She woke up early this morning. In a bad humour. A wave of bronze hair fell over her eyebrows and she brushed it back with her long fingernails.

"It's late."

I swung my legs out of bed, grabbed my denim skirt and slid into it. I slipped my brown embroidered vest over my faded green shirt.

"Coming?" I remembered Lindsay was looking for work. She had been laid off the week before from her job as a salesgirl at a specialty boutique that was closing its doors. I wanted to give her a ride to the nearest shopping centre where she could apply for a job. I drank some milk and put the carton back inside the fridge. "Coming with me?"

"Where? Nowhere to go." She clamped her hair back and tied it into a ponytail.

"You could look for something at the mall."

"Awww. . . right. Think it's a bit too early. The mall's not open. I'll go later."

"With the bus?"

"Guess so." She snapped a crescent moon barrette on top of her ponytail. "Maybe I'll walk. Or I'll get a ride."

"With Kerry?"

"That's my best chance. Kerry's always helpful. Hope I'll find something soon, or I won't have any money for the rent."

"Don't worry about the rent. I'm working. I'll get paid."

"If you can keep your job."

She is nasty when she is in a bad mood. I wish I could help her out, but I know she wouldn't enjoy staying locked up inside an office all day long. Lindsay prefers to deal with people. She'd rather work as a salesgirl for the cosmetics department at the Art Mart.

"I'd better hurry." I just started working at Corral Computers as a receptionist. My boss warned me there might be a visitor, a buyer from out of town who might drop in early, and I must make sure he feels at home. Have to arrive at the office before he does, or the boss will fire me.

Outside, the freezing drizzle sprinkles my cheeks with chalky-white powder. I tug at the collar of my old coat. The hood is frazzled and the fake fur trim loses hair, but it will still keep me dry. As I pull my burgundy corduroy gloves on, my fingertips stick out, bare and pink like a litter of newborn baby mice.

I notice a flashy black motorcycle showing off its glossy chrome trimming by the neighbour's driveway. Did Kerry buy a motorbike? Strange, I hadn't noticed that motorcycle before. Saw him wrapped in a grease-stained overall when he worked on his blue Ford. He might have kept the black bike hidden inside his garage all winter. This motorcycle is similar to Khoren's. He used to spend hours fixing his hog back home. Bet he would be lost here in the city. Wouldn't know where to find the parts for his motorbike. Or how to cope with road rage. I can't forget how he'd stared at me when he took me for my first ride ever. I'm still not sure if it was a pass or a compliment.

My Datsun is parked by the curb. I stare at the frost petals stuck to my windows. Can't help but glance inside. No mean Ripper curled up on the back seat with a knife. I've heard about a girl who was attacked as she got out of her car in a parkade downtown. No one heard her scream. The attacker wrapped her scarf around her mouth. Choked her. Left her unconscious with a livid ring around her neck. It was the motorist who had been tailgating her earlier. He accused her of cutting him off at an intersection. He slapped her and punched her to get his way with her. The police found out he had a twin brother who shaved his head to look different. The skinhead had stalked that girl's sister before. When they went to court, the twins accused each other of assaulting the teen sisters. The judge had to postpone the case to find out who did what to whom.

I slip inside my car and I slide the key into the ignition. The engine rattles back to life. I switch the wipers on. They swish, sweeping the drizzle-encrusted windshield. Foamy as dribbling saliva, slushy rivulets drip along the sides of the windshield and melt at the bottom.

When I shift gears, the car jerks and sputters down the street. I feel my heart leap up to my throat. I step on the brake pedal. But my engine coughs and gasps. It wheezes. Sounds like it's choking. Has to warm up. The pistons knock and hammer with an uneven rhythm, sticks beating a drum under the vibrating hood.

As I push on the gas, my Datsun swerves. Can't step on the wrong pedal. My car coasts along the curb, leaving behind the brown bungalow where I live.

The front bumper is aiming for the motorbike. I stomp on the brake. Can't stop.

The tires are sliding on a thin coat of black ice. I skid to the intersection. Other motorists honk their horns. How am I going to get out of this one? I try to steer clear of all the other vehicles until the left fender noses into a mound of gravel and snow. Clunk. My Datsun spins around. Thud. It places its rear end at an awkward angle. Jolts to a halt, making my nerve ends tingle. The engine gurgles and dies. Stalled.

Must do something about it. Have to be at work on time, or I'll be in trouble. They're just trying me out, for heaven's sake. How could I call a tow truck? Too expensive. I don't have a cellular phone and can't leave my car here. With all the cuts at work, a girl must watch what she's doing. I don't earn much. But I can't afford to be out of a job. Have to support myself in this city. My mother told me not to leave home. Now, I have to look after myself. Have to stay away from Khoren. He could bother me again.

Swarthy and brawny, Khoren loved motorcycles. He had bought an old motorbike at an auction and when he found some free time, he would try to fix it. In summer, he took off his shirt in the hot sun and showed off the muscles on his back with the tattoo of a cougar opening its jaw wide, as if to chomp the head off an uncoiling rattlesnake.

Very early in the morning, when no one was around, Khoren would clean Haynk's barn. He shoveled mountains of manure and would often wear a large-rimmed felt hat that kept his face in the shadow, but his eyes still shone like two burning charcoals. His dark hair would rake across his strong neck. People didn't mind him until he pierced his left nostril with a silver hoop. They said he did it himself and his nostril became infected with pus. It turned purple and swelled up to twice its normal size.

One day as he was tiding up bales of hay in the barn, one of the mares stumbled over a loose board. It neighed and stomped outside, but found itself trapped within the corral. The horse snorted, its wet nostrils blowing steam. Khoren chased after it, waving his felt hat. The mare bucked and then stood on its hind legs, ready to trample on any obstacle. As the horse dropped down, one of its front hooves hit Khoren's shoulder. The man's legs buckled under the weight and they both fell. Khoren bumped his head against a stone and lost consciousness. When he came to, his legs were still pinned under the horse.

Khoren managed to free himself, but couldn't leave the mare lying on the ground. The horse would have to stand up, or it might get sick and die. Khoren found two sticks, tore off the sleeves of his shirt and tied them together to make a temporary splint for the animal's sprained leg.

At first, Haynk praised Khoren for saving his mare. But a few days later, he accused him of tripping Kleo on purpose, his best workhorse.

"You made Kleo fall. You *sunovabitch!*" The farmer yelled and shook his fist. "Did it on purpose, huh? To ruin me. Me and my cute white-freckled Kleo."

"Never would do such a thing! Why would I?" Khoren gasped. "You know me better than that, Haynk. I'd die for Kleo. Your favourite mare. Almost did."

"How dare you say that? Shit! If Kleo hears you . . . you're in trouble!" Haynk yelled.

"Kleo wouldn't mind." Khoren touched the ring on his

infected nostril. "Kleo listens to me."

"Hah, now I know why Kleo fell!"

"Why?"

"You were about to pierce Kleo's nostril and put a ring like yours through it. So you two could smooch." He scowled. "Thought I saw a needle sticking out of her nose."

"Didn't."

"Get out of here." Haynk went after Khoren with a hay fork. "Go away before I poke you one."

Khoren could never go back to work. No farmer would hire him after the nasty rumour about Kleo spread. Nobody would risk having their horses' nostrils pierced by Khoren. No one wanted him around. But he couldn't live forever on blueberries and dandelion wine. He grew as skinny as a twig and his biceps shrunk as he toiled to fix the old motorcycle he had bought. He even built some of the parts he needed himself. Yet no one believed he could make the spluttering engine run until he managed to start it one day. He hopped onto the seat and went on a test drive, bouncing along a dusty country road. He crossed a lumpy field of summer fallow until he reached a berry hedge.

I was picking blueberries that grew huge like black marbles by a grove of leafy oaks when I heard his bike's sputtering motor. Khoren drove up, roaring closer to me. My heart sped up as the bike did a pop-a-wheelie. He was aiming straight for me. I jumped out of the way.

"Want a ride?" He grinned, braking hard. He stroked the rusty handlebar as if it were a pet.

I couldn't understand why he would ask me to hop onto his motorbike. Taller than most girls my age, I was too thin to attract a boy's attention. But I'd never tried riding a motorcycle before and I wanted to find out more about that. It looked like fun to me. I wasn't sure if my mother would approve, but I climbed onto the seat behind him. I put my arms around his shoulders and we took off.

I held on tight as we rode faster, skipping over the potholes along the gravel road. The wind blew in my hair, whistling unknown secrets in my ears. I tightened my grasp around Khoren who bent over his bike as if it were a feral boar jumping and galloping out of control. We sped past some yellow patches of mustard fields and my aching throat felt raw. We were heading for the village. What would my mother say if she saw me on Khoren's motorcycle? I would be grounded. I blinked and let the cool wind erase any unpleasant thoughts from my mind.

We zoomed through main street and roared nearer the grey stucco house where I lived. A few villagers gathered in front of the local bar. They glared at me, as if to warn me not to hang onto Khoren like that. I stretched out my arms, trying to stay away from him. But I almost slipped off the seat. I clutched his body tighter. He smelled like sweat and freshly cut hay.

Silhouetted in the doorway, my mother leaned against the wall and put her fist on her hip. She bared her teeth as Khoren started slowing down. I was frightened. The grimace on my mother's face scared me. A bad omen. I let go of Khoren and jumped off the motorbike.

I rolled on the dusty ground. I was sweating. Dazed. My head and my face hurt. My stomach churned faster than the windmill at the edge of the village. My yellow striped skirt was torn and stained with oil and grease. I didn't want my mother to see me like that. She would have a fit. But she rushed over and glared at me. I looked away. Couldn't get up. My legs felt like rubber. My arms were red with scratches. I wanted to run away. But I couldn't move.

"I told you to stay away from that man. Someone with

a ring in his nose is up to no good." She made me stand up and she slapped the dirt off my skirt. "Look at those stains. Won't be able to wash them away. What happened to your cheek? It's scratched. Is it cut?"

"Rape!" a neighbour shouted. "Get that rapist."

The enraged villagers stomped past us. "Rape!" Everyone yelled as they chased after Khoren who roared away without glancing back. "Let's get him. Look! His ring ripped Sarah's cheek. Body-piercer. Has a ring even on his navel! On his nose. On his tongue! His dink!"

Khoren sped along the road leading to Haynk's farm. Kleo was grazing by the ditch. The mare raised its head and sniffed the air when it heard the motorcycle coming closer. The animal wheezed, leapt over the barbed wire fence and limped down to the creek for a drink of water.

Haynk clenched his fists, running in front of Khoren's motorcycle to flag him down. Khoren veered to the right to avoid the farmer. He went in the ditch. Haynk grabbed some stones and threw them at the zigzagging bike. A heavy shower of rough-edged rocks and gravel pounded Khoren as he bounced away on his bike. He never returned to Haynk's farm. Neither did Kleo. Haynk still misses his mare. He swears Khoren stole Kleo and sold it at an auction in some other village. Or he might have had the nerve to butcher Kleo. The gall. Like everyone else, I feel bad for the horse.

I push the inside door handle of my car. Stuck. Maybe frozen. In the rearview mirror, I see the black motorcycle shooting away from the neighbour's driveway. It speeds to the intersection where my car is stalled. Its front headlight glows and sparkles, as if made of live embers. A one-eyed Polyphemus. It doesn't slow down. The biker doesn't notice me. What can I do? I feel paralyzed. Can't get out of my car.

I wave my arm out of the window as a warning signal. But the evil eye aims at me. Becomes larger. Blinding bright. I can't even look at it. I tighten my grasp around the steering wheel, bracing myself for a collision. Bang! Clank.

I strike the steering wheel with my chest. My hands clutch the dashboard tighter. I am afraid to glance at the motorbike behind me. What am I going to do if the biker is hurt?

Someone is lying on the ground. It's a man in black jeans and black leather jacket. He writhes and kicks on the icy pavement. I manage to squeeze out of my car.

I have a hard time breathing. "Are you all right?" I help him get up.

"Ouch!" His chest is heaving. "Hell!" He is rubbing his stomach. "Jeeezzz!" He stumbles to his bent bike, grabs his yellow goggles, then he kicks the rear hubcap of my car.

"Don't," I say.

"Bejezzuzz!" He hobbles around. "Don't know how to drive yet, huh?"

"Sure do!"

"Look at what you've done!" he scolds me and shoves back his black helmet. "The impact could have split my cranium. Cut my throat. Decapitated me."

"Didn't mean to." My face is becoming hot as if I were standing near a furnace.

"You didn't, huh? See this?" He points to the front wheel of his motorbike. "It's damaged. Some spokes broke off. Need repairs." As the man shakes his fist under my nose, I notice a ring piercing his left nostril. "You shouldn't leave that wreck of yours in the middle of the intersection."

"It stalled. You didn't have to hit me." I clench my fists. *Don't want to back away. I must stand my ground.*

"You could have pushed that bitch of a car out of the

way. Why didn't you?"

"Didn't have enough time."

"A motorcycle can't slow down all of a sudden, like a car does. Especially on icy roads. That wreck of yours could have drilled through me, piercing my body." He steps closer to me and waves his fist near my chin. "You should have flashing yellow lights to warn other motorists."

My mouth feels dry as if it were full of glue. Can hardly move my lips. "Don't have flashing lights."

"Should get yourself a lawyer." He pokes my side with his elbow. "You're lucky I'm not dead." He strokes his black helmet. His face has the pale yellow colour of salted butter. "Real lucky."

"So are you." As he twists to one side, I focus on the silver ring clamped on his nostril. His nose ring is like the one Khoren wore.

He pulls out a knife from his riding boot. "Do you want to get your face messed up?"

"It's no use talking to you. Be sensible." *Can't show him I'm afraid, or things might get worse. I'm on my own.* Other drivers speed by and don't care about my troubles.

"Give me your insurance number. Have to pay for my motorcycle, you know."

"You bumped into me. You have to give me the name of your insurance too." I fumble in my purse to find the pink card I always carry with me.

He slides his knife back into its sheath in his riding boot, jots down the name and number printed on my pink card. "Going to the gas station?"

"Wish I could." The bumper of my Datsun is scratched. "Can't even get the car started."

"Is it flooded?"

"No. Don't think so."

"We'll find out soon enough." He takes his helmet off. His reddish hair is pressed down like a copper cap pasted to his scalp. A silver hoop sparkles on his left lobe.

I open the door of my car. "Wasn't your bike parked on the street today, near that brown bungalow over there?" I motion down the street.

"Yeah! Just visiting the city for a few days. I stay with my cousin Kerry a couple of blocks down." He drags his bike closer to the curb and he kicks at its crooked stand. "Drat! Have an important meeting this morning. Don't need this trouble." He takes his cellphone from his side pocket and punches in a few numbers. "I'm stuck at the intersection. Yeah! Got to hurry." He nods at his cellphone.

"Work?" I ask him.

He bends over, trying to straighten out his front wheel. "Can't be late." He stabs at the chrome spikes.

"Same here. Have to get to work."

"Let's see if we can start that wreck of yours. Unless you want to ride on my bike at your own risk." He shrugs, pulls up my car hood and fiddles with the battery cables.

"I'd rather not ride on your bike." From the back trunk, I take out a shovel and I clear away the slush around the tires. I always carry a bag filled with sand. I spread some sand on the ground to allow the tires to get a good grip.

The biker slams shut the hood of my Datsun and nods to me. "A battery cable was loose and I tightened it. Try starting your car now and see if it works."

I sit behind the steering wheel and turn the key. The engine sounds groggy. Sleepy. Cranky. It wakes up with a loud gasp and catches on with a roar.

I drive past the intersection. In the rearview mirror I watch the blue Ford pull up to the black motorcycle. It's Kerry in his green hooded parka.

A familiar figure with a bronze ponytail gets out of the blue Ford. It's Lindsay. She's talking to the biker. Together, arm in arm, they walk to the bike. They'll have to take the motorbike to the body shop. It needs quite a bit of work.

It wasn't my fault. But my insurance will go up for sure. It's getting late and I step on the gas.

I screech to a halt in the parking lot behind the brick building where I work. Inside, a clerk is pecking away at the keyboard of her computer.

She twitches her eyebrows and stares at me. "About time! Did you meet the Ripper or something?" She sounds grouchy like Lindsay.

"Don't remind me." I take my coat off.

"What happened to you? You look kind of pale."

"Had some trouble getting to work," I murmur and turn to face the monitor. The screen forms tiny snowflakes, a drizzle of pixels shaping a puzzle of letters and numbers.

The entrance door to Corral Computers swings open and a man in tight black jeans and leather jacket steps in. He has a ring on his left nostril.

Can this be true?

It's him. The motorcyclist who earlier bumped into me. Is he the visitor the boss expected? Sure hope he forgot we met before and doesn't bring it up here at work.

Don't know how I am going to handle this, but I'm sure I'll have to deal with anything he may come up with. Later, Lindsay may let me know what he said to her about me.

Maybe she'll get her nose and ears pierced. She told me Kerry wants her to wear at least two silver rings on one nostril and three on the right lobe. If she finds a job, she'll get a ride in his blue Ford. I'm sure Kerry won't mind.

I go home for lunch, but can't find Lindsay. She left me a note. "*Just trying out the bike. See if it works. Yeah! With*

Kerry's cousin. The front wheel is still shaky. Beryl says you bumped into each other on the way to work. Lindsay."

Bet she'd like to move out of town with Beryl. He's younger and better looking than Kerry. First, his motorbike scraped the bumper of my car and wrecked my life and now, he's trying to get my friend Lindsay to travel and live in another city with him.

She must decide on her own. If she doesn't mind Beryl and his bike, and wants to have a rough ride, that's fine with me.

PIPESTONE

His silhouette etched against a darkening sky, Ozzie
kicked a rock out of the way and stared at several blustery
thunderheads chasing after one another. The dark horns
pushed, poked and shoved each other like snorting buf-
faloes, stampeding until they would fall off the cliff of the
horizon. The wind moaned and rust-veined leaves shivered and rustled on aspen branches. Blades of grass bent over,
seeking shelter closer to the ground. Ozzie kept walking
along the brook with Shock. They headed into the storm.

Ruddy-faced, Ozzie would toil hard all year-round and
he often forecasted the weather. Aunt Sylvia would always
seed her garden according to his predictions. He could fore-
tell whether wheat, mustard, corn, oats or canola should be
sown to yield the best crop each year. But he couldn't fore-
see the omen of what was about to happen.

Talking about Ozzie would make Aunt Sylvia bite the
head off the gingerbread boy she just baked. She would gulp
down all her coffee at once. "Too hot!"

She couldn't blame Ozzie for beating his head against
the wall, swearing to get even with Mudd and Gottfried
soon. Mudd lived on the farm on one side of the gravel road
which led to Kyle's house not far from the brook. Mudd was
a hard-working man with chafed-red hands and grime-
rimmed nails. He would always laugh loud at the local bar.

But every time he would glance at Kyle's daughter Kim, his mouth opened and his dark pupils widened as if he had never seen a girl before.

During the hot summer months, he used to climb up a spindly oak tree at dusk and, perched like a hawk on a leafy limb, he would aim his binoculars at Kim's window. He tried to watch her let her long hair down, but she would draw her curtains shut before undressing.

One moonless night, Kim listened to the brook murmur nature's mystery below her window. Crickets shrieked and fireflies dotted the night air. Mudd crept along the exterior brick veneer of the house. He lassoed the chimney with a rope and started climbing up to Kim's windowsill.

Her father heard some scratching and creaking on the south wall of his house. Armed with his hoe, he rushed out.

"Rotten! Bastard!" Kyle yelled. "Get down here. Rat. Right now!" He tugged at the rope. Mudd jerked his head back as the unknotted rope slipped from the chimney. He fell to the ground with a thud.

"Hey!" Mudd touched his sore hip. With both hands, he tried to fend off the striking hoe. "Don't."

"Bastard. You and Gottfried blowing up oil wells."

"Wait. I'll get my cat," Mudd shouted back.

"What's your cat going to do?"

"Fix you up."

"You can't fix anything." Kyle shrugged. "But sure can muddle things up though." He caught the rope with his hoe and twisted it tighter around the writhing Mudd.

"Humphhh! Watch what you're doing."

"Get away! Don't want you here."

"Why do you tie me up then?" Mudd sat up, untangling the rope around his body. "You complain. Not Kim."

"Leave my dear daughter out of this." He chased Mudd

along the thick caragana hedge by Pipestone Brook feeding Thistle Creek. But Mudd escaped into the night.

Next morning, Kim groomed her horse in the corral she had built with her own hands. Her long hair was combed back and tied into a braided ponytail matching the fringes of her sleeves. The smooth, tanned skin on her face made her look calm and relaxed as if she could never get mad. She whispered in Mait's ear, stroking its brown mane, when Mudd showed up on the other side of the fence.

"Hi!" he called out to her. But she didn't look up at him. Didn't stop grooming her horse. "Jump over the fence. The grass is greener here. Life's better here with me."

He grinned, climbed on the fence and rode the top log as if it were a horse. He took off his belt and flogged the log. "Whoaa! Yaoooh!" The belt hissed close to Mait's head.

Kim ducked behind Mait. "Don't you dare lash out at my horse!" she shouted. She gripped Mudd's belt and tugged hard.

Mudd slid off the fence. "What are you trying to do?" He smirked. "Do you want me that bad?"

She punched him with her fists. "Get away!" She took a deep breath as she saw Ozzie rushing up to them.

Ozzie shoved Mudd back. "Don't you dare touch her!" he shouted.

"But you can, huh?" Mudd shook his fist, spun the belt high above his head like a propeller and lunged forward. He barely missed Ozzie's nose.

"Let us be," Ozzie warned him. "Go away."

"Not bothering anyone." Mudd flogged the air again with his belt, but the horse stood up on its hind legs and neighed. Its nostrils shivered, sending out feathers of steam. A hoof smacked Mudd in the chest as he stumbled back. "Beast! You damned animal!" He leaned against the fence and rubbed his chest.

"Sweet with my sister Daisy's kid, Sasha, but real tough with bullies like you," Ozzie said as Mait whinnied and flattened the grass with its stomping hooves.

"*Sunuvabitch!*" Mudd touched his ribs with his fingers. "Could have broken a rib."

"Don't say that! You're making my horse nervous," Kim scolded.

"I'll kick its rear end. That's what I'll do," Mudd rasped, but didn't dare move closer to Mait.

Mait snorted and stomped on the ground as if to test the strength of a troublesome opponent.

"Don't you bother that poor horse!" Ozzie screamed, clenching his fists.

"Sore loser!" Mudd spat near Mait's hooves. He hammered the corral fence with his fists. "I'll have to kick you back. You and your owner, who can't teach you how to behave. I can give you both a lesson you'd never forget."

"No, you won't." Ozzie scowled.

"I'll have to pay a visit to your sister Daisy. Tell her how bad you are. She understands."

Ozzie grabbed Mudd's thick neck and squeezed hard. "No way. You're rotten. Rotten to the core."

Mudd gasped. "Let go of me." He jerked back, shoved Ozzie against the corral gate. "You'll pay for that. To hell!" He swore and hurried away across the field to his farm.

At harvest time, Ozzie tried to forget about Mudd and he toiled in the field under the hot sun. Kim would bring him ham sandwiches and cool apple juice. She also baby-sat little Sasha for his sister Daisy, a single mother who could never hold a job for too long. Ozzie didn't have the heart to send her away. He wanted to give her a hand, but he often wished she could help herself. He worked hard to keep a roof over their heads. He had to pay the mortgage for the farm. If he didn't harvest a good crop of wheat and corn, he would have to sell a couple of cows to come up with the cash. Soon, he discovered how hard it is to repay a loan. It would never shrink and seemed to grow like a weed.

When Ozzie applied for a job in the oil business to earn some extra money, there was nothing available. He had to work his butt off on his farm and get what he could out of those eighty acres of land near Pipestone Brook.

Daisy couldn't agree with a stubborn man like her brother. He never spoke about what bothered him. Ozzie would sit at the table and gnaw the meat off a rib bone, swallowing fast without saying a word. She placed the gravy bowl on the table, her lean arm stretched out. Her hips were wrapped in her frayed denim skirt. She chose tough material, but she had to wear her denims for far too long.

Under stress, the worry lines on her forehead multiplied. She often toiled hard for meager pay. She kept a garden and took care of the brand new litter of Siamese kittens for Gottfried Khoner, their neighbour, to earn some spending money. But at times, when Gottfried was not working on a job in town or as a volunteer fireman, she would get paid only with a few carrots and tomatoes.

"Once you start farming, you have to only look ahead. Can't go back. Seed early in the spring what you want to grow, or you won't get another chance to do it," Daisy told Ozzie as if she knew everything about farming. She would put her palm under her strong chin to underline her words.

"Easy for you to say," Ozzie swallowed some beer from a can and belched. "You just plant tomato seedlings."

Daisy frowned. "If you could get along with your neighbours, it might pay off."

"Like who? Mudd? Gottfried? Who can get along with

everyone around here?"

"People like Mudd and Gottfried could help."

"Shut up." He drained the can and tossed it into the trash box. "Silly. Terrorists. Selfish people!"

"Look! Sounds like you know a lot about Mudd already." Daisy served her brother more mashed potatoes and ribs. "At least he doesn't pretend to be what he's not."

Ozzie chewed on the meat and his lips became greasy as he ate. "Whose side are you on anyway? His?" He glared at Daisy. "Like the guy, or something? I'll kill him anyway."

"What a hard-headed moron you are!" She turned and spooned more gravy onto his mashed potatoes. "Here. It's for your own good, Ozz."

"Sure. If he ever bothers you, I'll kick his ass."

"He doesn't harass me."

One day, when Ozzie went to eat a bite at *Beans and Razzberries* earlier that summer, he discovered he didn't have enough money for an egg sandwich and beer. Mudd lent him a few bucks and asked Ozzie to give him a hand building his new porch.

They started out by nailing two-by-fours together to make the wooden frame. They planned to put up the first wall next day, but during the night the plywood stored in Mudd's backyard went missing. Mudd became enraged and accused Ozzie of stealing his plywood.

"Where's my plywood?" he asked gruffly. "I want it all back. Where did you put all that stuff?"

"Don't know where it is." Ozzie stepped away.

"Damn thief! Took even the two-by-four frames that were nailed together. Stupid! Rabid dog!" Mudd poked Ozzie's chest with his index finger.

"Wouldn't even take a single nail from you." Ozzie

grimaced. His ruddy face looked harsher when he raised his bristly eyebrows.

"Give me back what belongs to me."

"Sure thing. How could I give you back something I never took?"

"Don't play dumb." He raised a claw hammer above his head. Ozzie blocked his arm before Mudd could hit him.

"We can search together for your plywood."

"Let's go take a look on your farm." Mudd pouted. He broke a pine branch and kicked a cow pie with the metal tip of his black boot.

They both searched around Ozzie's farm, inside the wooden shed, by the chicken coop and past a pyramid of manure. But there was no sign of Mudd's plywood on Ozzie's farm.

"Can't find your stuff around here." Ozzie kicked a rake out of the way. "That's because I didn't take it."

"That's what you'd like me to believe."

"What do you mean?"

"Bet you sold my plywood already, huh?" Mudd shook one fist near Ozzie's jaw. "So, I wouldn't find it anywhere, not even on your farm."

Ozzie grunted. "No."

Mudd hit him with a powerful blow. Ozzie staggered for a moment, but regained his balance and fought back. He struck out at Mudd's chin and punched his nose hard until it started bleeding. Mudd went crazy when he saw blood staining his shirt. He lowered his head like a goat set out to poke someone's butt. But when he saw Daisy run out of the house with Kim, he froze. Daisy tore off the white cotton apron she wore while baking cherry turnovers.

"Stop this nonsense, Ozzie!" she screamed. "Shame on you both." She tugged hard at her brother's arm. "Stop!"

Ozzie shrugged. "I didn't start all this trouble."

"You sure did." Mudd turned to Daisy. "Your brother stole my plywood."

"I'd know if he did," Daisy said. "And I'd return what belongs to you."

Mudd kicked some dirt and scared a squawking hen. "How could my plywood disappear overnight?"

Daisy bowed her head and sighed. "Think I saw some kids building a tree house by the ravine. Not far from the brook."

"Is that true?"

"They had some plywood and two-by-fours."

"I'll get that lazy brother of yours. He has to bring back all my plywood so I can finish my porch." Mudd stamped his footprints in the plowed field as he headed back to his farm.

"What is Mudd up to?" Daisy wondered.

"Nothing good." Ozzie grimaced. He glanced at Kim and looked up at the sky as if he could learn his fate.

They watched Mudd stomp to the side of his log barn where a corn yellow caterpillar was parked. He climbed up, sat in the driver's seat and started the engine. When he shifted gears, the cat pounced ahead leaping over large stones protruding from the black soil.

As Mudd drove back to the corral, Sasha scampered out of the house. "Sasha! Wait." Daisy stretched out her arms and ran after her two-year-old. But Sasha waved his chubby arms and scuttled away on his wobbly little legs.

"Daisy! Sasha." Ozzie yelled. "Watch out!" he warned, but they kept on running.

"Sasha!" Daisy called out again to the toddler who giggled as the tractor bounced over piles of stones. It headed for them but it was just a game for Sasha. He watched the cat's front loader rake through the furrows.

The wind gusts made the tree branches whistle and a thunderclap shook the ground. Kim hopped onto her horse and tightened the reins. "Let's get him, Mait. Hurry!" The horse snorted galloping toward the tractor.

"Watch out for the cat. Wouldn't want you or Mait to get hurt," Ozzie yelled. The yellow cat rumbled ahead, its headlights glaring. The horse was gaining ground and didn't seem to be scared. But Mudd's caterpillar leapt over black clumps of dirt like a tank threatening to wipe out anything that might stand in its way.

As the roar of the diesel engine became deafening, Mait began acting up. It grunted and trampled the ground with its hooves. Backing up onto its hind legs, the horse threw Kim off the saddle with a sudden jerk.

She hit her head on a tree stump and she didn't get up. Ozzie rushed to her and knelt beside her on the grass by the caragana hedge. As blood oozed from a deep gash on her brow, he tore off his shirt sleeves to bandage her head.

Mait trotted closer to Sasha, circling clumps of poison ivy and sniffing the danger in the air.

Scrambling over a mound of stones, Sasha could run fast on his short legs. "Watch out for that big horse!" Daisy screamed. "It runs faster than the tractor."

Sasha giggled. He used to play near Mait's hooves without fear. He loved horse riding with Kim and often he tried to climb up on Mudd's caterpillar as if it were a big fun toy to sit on and drive.

Not far away from the toddler, the front loader nuzzled the ground and aimed at Sasha who waved his hands in excitement.

"Maw!" he shouted and pointed at the caterpillar.

Daisy's face turned livid. "Stay away! It will hurt you. The big tractor will crush you!"

The yellow loader stuck out from the cat like the huge mouth of a hippopotamus about to gobble everything.

Mait galloped past the cluster of poison ivy and lurched across the path of the caterpillar, waiting to fight the steel-mouthed monster.

Mudd halted the cat with a big jolt, the loader's arm bashing against Mait's tail. He jumped out of the cabin and banged his head on the steel roof. "Ouch!" he shouted. Mait clobbered the cat's front loader with its hooves. But when the animal bucked closer, Mudd ran away.

"That Mudd's crazy!" Ozzie yelled. He picked up Sasha and handed him over to Daisy who hugged him.

"What about poor Kim?" Daisy wondered. She watched Ozzie bend over the unconscious girl. He couldn't revive Kim and Daisy called an ambulance.

Sprawled on the ground not far from the brook, Kim reminded him of his former girlfriend Tara who was hit by a bullet as she was riding her bicycle along the nature path cutting through the ravine near Thistle Creek.

The hunter's fatal shot wasn't intended for her, but for a partridge hiding behind the trunk of a mountain ash. Trouble was, Tara was pregnant. Ozzie rushed her to the nearest hospital and the doctors attempted a Cesarean delivery, but couldn't save their baby.

"Why would an innocent cyclist have to pay for some-body else's mistake?" Ozzie couldn't figure that one out. He didn't believe in fate. He thought we could decide our own destiny, choosing what to do in life. "If only she wouldn't have biked along Thistle Creek ravine."

He blamed himself for not being able to help Tara and their baby. Later on in despair, he sliced his wrists with a razor blade and Daisy rushed into the bathroom where she found him unconscious in a pool of blood. She bandaged his wrists, stopped the bleeding and called Kim to help out. At the hospital, Kim let Ozzie have some of her blood. She was the only one around with the O-positive type which could be given safely even to those who have different types of blood. Both Daisy and Kim nursed Ozzie back to health.

After the fall off her horse that day, Kim lost a lot of blood from the gash on her brow. She needed a blood transfusion. Ozzie had the best blood match for her. The medics didn't lose any time and wheeled Kim into the operating room. Later on, when Kim awoke, she couldn't remember what happened.

"Am I pregnant or something?" she asked, touching her stomach.

"What if you were? Want to get married?" Ozzie winked at her and touched her hand. He didn't want to tell her yet about the blood transfusion. It went well and he didn't have to worry. He stared at the purple veins pulsating on her wrist and he felt she was really part of him. Or was he part of her?

She sighed and looked around. "Where is Mait?"

"Went to the vet for a checkup and a vitamin shot. Now, Mait's back at home."

She propped herself onto her left elbow. "How is my favourite rancher doing?"

"Just needs the best girl in town."

Kim smiled. "Daisy okay?"

"Looking after things out at the farm. Lots of work." He grinned. "Sasha's her little helper. Can you imagine?"

Ozzie hugged her and left. He went back to work on his farm and he helped Kim's father to clean the stable and shovel mounds of manure.

Daisy still looked after the new litter of blue-eyed Siamese kittens for Gottfried Khoner, but she was concerned about Mudd. She had not seen him for a long time. His tractor still stood abandoned in the field. People saw Mudd picking berries near another village. Fruit growers chased him away from their apple orchards. They gossiped about Mudd's sharp cheekbones protruding under dark-circled eyes which lacked sleep.

Walking along the brook, Ozzie didn't have to worry anymore about Mudd bothering Kim or Daisy. He took his hound Shock with him and let him roam around without the leash.

He lost the dog one day when a bulky man showed up at the opposite end of the footpath. Ozzie stepped over the rocks of the creek bed and almost lost his balance.

"Trying to go for a swim, huh?" It was Gottfried, the part-time firefighter who hired Daisy to raise the Siamese kittens. Everyone called him Poison Ivy down at *Beans and Razzberries* where he gulped down chicken soup with egg sandwiches. He would often display his crooked burnt-black fingernails and brag about how he had been branded when putting out a forest fire not far from the village. But other people said it was just his own barbecue that caught on fire and burned his apron and pants. "A swim in the mud, huh?"

"Would you jump in the water after me?" Ozzie clenched his teeth. He stared at Gottfried who shrugged.

"Don't know. Maybe. Why are you talking to me like that? Having trouble or something?" His chunky body stood by a tree trunk as if it were part of a wooden sculpture.

"No." He glanced around. "Shock!" he called out to his dog. But there was no sign of the salt and pepper hound.

"Causing trouble, huh?"

"Hey, Gott! Don't give me any problems."

"Yeah! Go ahead. Ignore everything. Your debts too." Gottfried sneered.

"Sure. I'll worry about that. Who's going to pay any of my debts? Not you. That's for sure."

"Why should I? You got the money. Not me." Gottfried's face reddened and his nose became violet. "Mudd had to vouch for you. You didn't even have enough cash to pay for your beans at *Razzberries*. Told me about the loan he gave you. Didn't even bother to pay him back, huh?"

"Mind your own business. Helped him with his porch."

"Yeah! Didn't work out though."

"Too bad."

"Let's see if we can work things out between us." Gottfried grinned and elbowed Ozzie's ribs.

"Hummph! Like what?"

"We could pan for gold in the brook. Fish out nuggets. This big." Gottfried opened his hand. "They'd make us rich. If we could find a few gold nuggets, there might be a lot more where those came from."

Ozzie stabbed the dirt with his left heel. "It's hard work to look for something you might never find."

"*Good* for you." Gottfried slapped Ozzie's shoulder. "We could sweat it out together. I'd take care of pans and sluice boxes. Got my hose and knives."

"Need more than that."

"Like what?"

"New blood. Red. Vital. The kind you need to feel alive. Without extorting money from oil companies."

"Alive my ass." Gottfried shook his fist under Ozzie's chin. "They're asking for it. Down with pipelines!"

"Can't even raise your own Siamese kittens. You sell them and don't pay my sister, who looks after your pets." Ozzie gripped Gottfried's arm and pushed it behind him.

"Hey! Trying to break my arm?" Gottfried bared his crooked teeth. He grunted and wrenched his arm free and with a powerful blow, he hit Ozzie who fell to the ground.

Ozzie grasped Gottfried's legs and pulled him down. They both struggled and tumbled over the grass of the steep slope leading to the gravel bank along the rushing brook. Cool water sprayed them both as Gottfried bit Ozzie's neck.

A throaty growl spread through the air. Shock rushed down the path leading to the brook. Panting, the mongrel barked and bared its teeth.

"Get him, Shock!" Ozzie snarled. "Get him!"

Shock bit into Gottfried's pant leg and shook it.

"You crazy? Or what?" Kim was running along the winding footpath. She rushed over to them. "Break it up! Shock! Down! Down, Shock. Don't bite."

Shock growled. Kim grabbed Gottfried's arms and pulled him back up the embankment. "Ooops! Was about to shove Ozzie into the creek." Gottfried gasped, got hold of her long braided ponytail and pulled.

She freed herself. "Don't do that."

"Always bossing me around, huh? Don't do this. Don't do that. Women!" He slapped some wet grass off his baggy pants.

Ozzie was rubbing his blue-black eye. "Can't understand what's wrong with Gottfried." He patted Shock's ears.

"I don't know either." Kim buttoned up her silk shirt. In her lime-green cutoffs, she looked slimmer and younger than Tara used to.

"Imagine. Duhhh!" Gottfried grunted. He reached for Kim's ponytail again.

Ozzie snapped at him. "Keep your hands off her."

"Don't make so much fuss." She patted his back.

"Yeah! He has to stay away from you."

"Wait!" Gottfried pulled her back. "You stay away from Ozzie too."

"What's the trouble?" Ozzie paled. His heart gave him a jolt. Pain shot through his body.

"You'll get AIDS. You don't want that, Kim."

Ashen-faced, Ozzie raked through his messed-up hair with trembling fingers. "Why? What do you mean?"

Gottfried sighed. "I'm HIV positive."

"My neck. You bit me!"

Kim touched Ozzie's shoulder. "We'll find a way. Get a test. Gott might be lying. Who knows?"

"Can't take chances." Ozzie grimaced and his sturdy face became ashen. "You never know." His lips trembled. He turned around and clenched his fists, but he didn't punch Gottfried.

Large raindrops splashed to the ground as Kim stroked his arm. "Don't want to end up like Mudd."

Gottfried grinned. "He's HIV positive too. Couldn't you figure that one out?" He snapped his bulky fingers at Shock. "Even the dog might get it."

Shock licked its master's hand and glanced up. Ozzie's scratched Shock's furry neck.

Aunt Sylvia wipes her eyes. She gulps down more black coffee and peers out of the window.

Another storm is brewing. Aunt Sylvia doesn't bother following the weather forecast these days. She doesn't want to talk anymore. She just gazes past me and stares at the gurgling brook feeding Thistle Creek.